Climbing Heartbreak Hill

All it takes is the courage to start.

by

Joselyn Vaughn

Joselyn Vaughn

Climbing Heartbreak Hill
by Joselyn Vaughn
Published by Astraea Press
www.astraeapress.com

CLIMBING HEARTBREAK HILL
Copyright © 2013 JOSELYN VAUGHN
ISBN 13: 978-1492387244
ISBN: 149238724X
Cover Art Designed by Book Beautiful

For the Koffee Kuppe Ladies, No matter where we are, we will always be together in spirit.

In honor of all those affected by the tragedy at the 2013 Boston marathon. Your courage inspires us. Run on!

Chapter One

"Tara, I feel a bit off."

Tara Mansfield replaced the phone in its cradle and swung her chair around. Leslie Schultz, her boss, pressed her palm against her back, forcing her growing belly to strain against her tailored maternity shirt. She had given up trying to button her suit jacket over her baby bump a month before. Leaning against the door to her office, she said, "Something at lunch didn't agree with me."

"You should lie down. Your next appointment isn't for another twenty minutes." Tara double-checked the schedule for the accounting office. At the height of tax season, it was almost unheard of to have a twenty minute break. Luckily, they'd had a cancellation this morning. Leslie could use a rest.

Leslie nodded slowly, rubbing her fingertips along the bottom of her stomach. "If I didn't know better I'd think I was having menstrual cramps." She winced and hunched forward, clutching the door jamb with white knuckles. Tara dashed toward her, heels sliding on the tiled floor. She grabbed Leslie's arm and steered her toward the break room where there was a futon. Leslie's steps wavered until she sank onto

1

the cushion. "At least it comes and goes. Maybe I will lie down for a few minutes."

Color slowly infused Leslie's cheeks and Tara breathed a sigh of relief. Leslie couldn't be going into labor yet. She had more than a month to go, not to mention the three busiest weeks of tax season. They didn't have a contingency plan for the baby arriving this early. Leslie *had* to be having those fake contractions. What had Leslie's husband, Mark, called them? Braxton-Hicks? "Rest for a bit. I'll get you some water. It will pass."

Tara opened the refrigerator and pulled out a bottle of water. Leslie nodded and pulled her cell phone out of the pocket of her jacket. "I'll catch up on some emails while I'm resting."

"Uh-uh. Hand it over." Tara offered the water with one hand and held the other out for the device. "It doesn't count as resting if your eyes are open."

Leslie reluctantly placed the slim, black device in Tara's outstretched palm. "You're worse than Minnie."

Tara grinned. "If only I were that ballsy. Now put your feet up. At this pace, the Tenaples will be here before you close your eyes."

Tara returned to her desk and placed the phone on a stack of files, a little surprised Leslie relinquished it so easily. She must be absolutely exhausted. Tara couldn't imagine working all these hours and being pregnant, too. The phone had been glued to Leslie's palm since mid-January. It had her appointment schedule, email, and to-do lists. Leslie needed it to keep up with all their appointments and IRS filings for the tax season.

"Let me know as soon as they arrive," Leslie called from the break room. "No stalling like yesterday."

Tara had been the receptionist at Knotts Accounting since Leslie purchased the building and started her own accounting firm. Tara had started out answering the phones, but with

Leslie's encouragement, she had taken the tax preparation courses last winter so she could help with the straightforward returns. Leslie was trying to talk her into returning to college for an accounting degree, but Tara hadn't gotten past the gathering-information-about-programs stage yet. She couldn't imagine herself going back to school. She had never been college material, not after high school and definitely not twelve years later. The tax seminar had been a breeze, but college with its lectures, exams, and hours of studying… she'd never survive.

"Sure thing." Tara wiggled her mouse, and the tax return she was working on materialized on her computer screen. Leslie was the last person Tara would have ever expected to be friends with. Leslie was an accountant. She was smart, professional.

No one would mistake Tara for any of those. Until she had returned to Carterville, she'd been a cheerleader for a regional arena football team. Not exactly an intellectually challenging position, but the money was good and she had the right look until they altered the design of the uniforms.

She'd fallen into this position when Leslie's business had suddenly taken off, and it had worked out. Tara hadn't expected to actually like doing tax returns, but she seemed to have an affinity for numbers. The details weren't mind-numbing either. She enjoyed the procedures and order. Tara finished the 1040 and queued it to be reviewed before filing with the IRS that evening.

Tax season was the busiest time of year for accounting firms, and Tara believed Knotts Accounting was the busiest in the county. Their phones rang off the hook and they had a dozen walk-ins each day. Staying until well into the evening wasn't unusual, and Tara doubted she'd have any free evenings between now and April fifteenth. She hoped Leslie could keep up. Every day her boss looked more sleep-deprived, but she refused to take even an afternoon or a

Saturday off.

The third week of March was the calm before the final storm. The people who expected a refund had already filed. The procrastinators and the people who knew they owed money to the government didn't make appointments until April. As it was, Tara's calendar was almost full, and they were trying to squeeze in every customer they could between now and the deadline. Tara and Leslie were enjoying this small reprieve as much as they could.

Mark had made Leslie go home at six every night this week. He'd had to physically drag her out of the office while she shoved papers into her briefcase. Last night he'd come close to tossing the leather case back in the office and throwing her over his shoulder. He'd tried to make her take a longer lunch today, but he might as well have held the negotiation with his hammer. Despite their reprieve, this week was crazy busy; next week would be frenzied.

Tara suspected Leslie wasn't resting as much as she should, given her May fifteenth due date, but she claimed she felt fine. Energized even. Until today, that is.

"Tara!" Leslie called from the back room. Her voice held a frantic tone Leslie never used.

Tara flipped her chair over as she dashed down the hall. Leslie braced herself on the edge of the futon. Her back ramrod straight and her face pale.

"Are you all right?"

"Could you call Mark? I'm pretty sure I just had a real contraction, and it was a doozy." If it was possible for Leslie's body to stiffen anymore, it did. She blew out long, slow breaths through clenched teeth. Then her body sagged. "It's way too early for this."

"Are you sure it's not those fake ones?" Tara dropped on the futon beside her. She rubbed Leslie's shoulders in a slow, circular motion.

"If that was fake, the real thing will kill me." Leslie

4

slumped against the back of the futon, shifting her hips to a reclining position. Leslie never slouched.

Tara hurried to her desk and grabbed the mobile handset, glad they'd upgraded the phones last fall. She pressed Mark's preset number and waited for him to answer.

"Hi Mark. This is Tara. Leslie had a contraction." The words tumbled out. Tara knew Mark wouldn't care that the message wasn't polite.

"I'm coming." Tara thought she heard his work truck engine flare before he hung up.

She didn't let go of the phone after hearing the dial tone. She wasn't sure what to do. Should she call the hospital? Minnie, Mark's aunt? Leslie's doctor? Leslie seemed awfully calm for a woman going into labor two months early, but she handled crises stoically. If Tara had been in her position, she would have been hysterical. People three blocks away would be able to time her contractions.

"Mark's on his way. Can I get you anything?"

Leslie's lips tightened. "If you have an epidural stashed in your desk, I'll take it straight up. Although if I have another contraction, I'm going to ask you to knock me out with a volume of the tax code."

Tara squeezed Leslie's shoulder. The bell on the front door rang, and Tara scurried down the hallway, wondering how Mark was able to arrive so quickly. But it wasn't Mark.

A lanky, sandy haired man on crutches elbowed his way through the door, alternating between pushing the glass door open and inching his crutches forward. He wore a red windbreaker with *Lakeshore Track Club* embroidered on the chest. Clutched between his left hand and the handle of his crutch was a wad of papers. It wasn't the worst presentation of receipts she'd seen in the last three months, but it would make the top ten.

She experienced a brief wave of déjà vu. A flash of his face laughing in the dark. Had she seen him before somewhere? His physique didn't match any of the football players she had been in contact with. Surely the strange bend in his nose would stand out enough in her memory. It gave him a reckless air she found appealing.

"Let me help you with that." She hurried over to the door and kicked the stopper down to hold it open while she relieved him of the fistful of paper. A quick scan of the parking lot told her Mark's truck hadn't arrived yet. "Do you have an appointment?"

"Your sign said walk-ins were welcome." His voice had a pleasant timbre. Tara didn't miss the once-over he gave her. She was used to those. It was one of the side-effects of having breast implants not written in the tri-fold brochure from the plastic surgeon: every male and one in three females will stare at your chest. At times, Tara wanted to wear a name-tag that said 'and yes, they are fake' under her name.

"Walk-ins are always welcome. We have a small break in the rush right now, so why don't you have a seat by my desk?" Tara released the door then made her way around her desk and righted her chair.

The man put the two crutches together and gingerly lowered himself into the seat. He kept his left leg extended, and Tara could see the outline of a brace around his knee through his warm-up pants. She dropped the pile of receipts into the middle of her desk and opened a new client file on her computer.

"Have you been here before?" When he answered in the negative, Tara said, "Okay. Then we'll need to go through the basics first. I'll need all your vital stats."

"Excuse me?"

"Name, address, phone number, etc."

"Oh, I thought you meant age, weight, heart rate, and blood pressure. Guess I've been to too many doctors lately. Ryan Grant." He rattled off an address she recognized as one of the Ladies Night Out members. Had Yvonne been holding out on her? They owed her a favor after she had helped them get Leslie and Mark together. The last names matched so he must be family. Perhaps Yvonne's son?

"Are you new in town then?" she asked as she typed the previous information into his record.

"At least until my knee heals." He rubbed the thigh muscle on the injured leg. "Had to move back in with my mom for a while. How embarrassing is that?" He flashed a grin that made Tara's stomach swirl.

"Not embarrassing at all." Considering she'd done the same three years before.

The doorbell jangled and Tara looked up, hoping for Mark. Instead, the Tenaples shuffled in, the next scheduled appointment. Mrs. Tenaple clutched a manila folder. Mr. Tenaple looked like he faced a colonoscopy. Tara didn't blame him. Their tax return was one of the most complicated in Carterville. Multiple 1099s, rental properties, and a monstrosity of a health savings account.

Leslie poked her head out of the break room. "Hello," she said through gritted teeth. "Let's go into my office." She took a step into the hallway as another contraction struck. Her knees buckled, and she slumped against the wall. Tara flew out of her chair, sending it spinning into her desk. She clutched Leslie's arm, urging her back to the break room. "Mark will be here any second. I'll reschedule the Tenaples."

"You can't. They always forget stuff. They'll be back and forth six times between now and the fifteenth. Do the pre-interview, and get their forms and fill out what you can," Leslie said between hitched breaths. "We get to the hospital, and I'm signing that stupid consent form for the epidural. If these are the practice ones, there's no way I'll survive the real thing."

Fill out what I can? The Tenaples' last return was an inch thick. All those deductions and 1099s. She'd barely get past their names and Social Security numbers. Tara gripped Leslie's elbows, trying to support her as much as fight the panic lurking in her chest. She couldn't handle the Tenaple's tax return. Leslie couldn't entrust that to her.

Then she looked into Leslie's face, and felt like the biggest idiot. She was complaining about paperwork when Leslie looked ready to cut this baby out with a letter opener.

The front bell rang again. Mark, in jeans and a T-shirt with his work belt still slung around his hips, zipped around the Tenaples and flew down the hall, his work boots leaving dusty footprints on the ceramic tiles.

"I grabbed your bag from home. That's why it took me so long. I'm on hold with the doctor. Let's go." He swept Leslie off her feet despite her protestations that she was the size of a small hippopotamus and could walk fine. Tara knew they were half-hearted; Leslie had struggled to make it two feet down the hallway.

The Tenaples gaped as Mark whisked Leslie around them and out the door. Tara stood behind her desk, one hand on her chair with three sets of eyes on her.

She was here alone with customers waiting. Customers who needed their taxes done. Customers who were depending on her. Her fingers dug into the mulberry upholstery. This wasn't what they planned. She couldn't handle this.

"Where's she going?" Mr. Tenaple asked as Mark's truck peeled out of the parking lot.

"Hospital," Tara replied, hoping her terror wasn't evident in her voice. "She's in labor." Even if Leslie's doctor managed to stop her contractions, they probably wouldn't let her return to work full-time. She couldn't see a doctor prescribing anything but bed rest. Without it and a pair of shackles, Leslie wouldn't stop overdoing it.

What am I going to do? She wanted to sink into the corner and throw a pity party with a whole orchestra of tiny violins. This wasn't what they planned. No wonder Minnie had laughed at them. Babies have their own schedule.

Tara remembered the customers in front of her. She had to fake competence. A strategy, that's what she needed. Something to get her through the next few minutes. She swallowed. Take care of these two customers, then she could reschedule the rest of the afternoon.

"Ryan, if you don't mind, I'll take the Tenaples' information and papers, then come back to you."

"Sounds fine to me. I'm in no hurry." He settled back in the chair while Tara led the Tenaples into Leslie's office. She pulled up their file on the computer and proceeded to verify their contact information.

She and Leslie had developed a contingency plan for when the baby was supposed to come. Her due date was May fifteenth, a full month after the tax season ended. But neither of them anticipated the baby coming almost two months early. Tara could handle most everything by herself through the summer months. For situations she couldn't — like quarter-end or year-end, Leslie had an accountant friend who would be able to fill in on a client by client basis. But right now with the three busiest weeks of the tax season left, Tara would be in trouble if she was on her own. There were returns she didn't have the expertise for. It would be a disaster.

Tara filled out as much of the Tenaples' information as she could and explained the situation to them. They understood and wondered if they should take their return somewhere else so as not to burden Knotts Accounting. Tara assured them she and Leslie would be able to complete the return, although she wasn't sure what she was basing her confidence on.

Chapter Two

Ryan Grant eased his leg into a more comfortable position. His knee ached in every position today. It would be better lying stretched out on the couch in front of the television, but he'd rather hang out in this stiff office chair than at home with his mother and her weird friends. He could face a thirty-mile run without flinching, but his mom and her friends were all hopped up about something. No way he was hanging around when they were scheming. Getting his taxes done, though painful and necessary, was a preferable option.

He scanned the desk in front of him and found the woman's nameplate tucked against the back of her flat screen. Tara Mansfield. He'd always had an affinity for the name Tara. Once, he'd had a run-in with a girl named Tara. It hadn't ended well on his end. He hoped she'd fared better, but he never saw her again. Every time he met another Tara, he remembered the gorgeous blonde and wondered what had happened to her.

This Tara was certainly eye-catching. He'd been staring at her curvaceous figure like an adolescent schoolboy. Couple that with the sunlit blond hair and sapphire blue eyes, and she had all the makings of a swimsuit cover model.

And yet, she was here in sleepy, old Carterville in an accounting office filing 1040s, wearing an ill-fitting business suit. There was probably a story behind that. He shifted his leg again. Her story was probably as pathetic as his own.

The office around him had been recently renovated with warm purples and fresh greens. Despite the functional look of the chairs, they accommodated his tall frame. Off in a corner was a small, primary-colored table with a box of toys and puzzles arranged next to it. The room Tara had led the couple into was glassed in. Blinds could be drawn to create privacy. She'd left the blinds open, and while he tried not to be obviously nosey, his attention kept focusing on how she interacted with the couple.

He could tell she was struggling to hide her nerves. As she talked to them, her hands flitted from straightening the papers in front of her to slipping the clasp of her necklace to the back of her neck to situating the mouse on its pad. He supposed having a boss about to deliver a baby upset one's schedule.

It wasn't long before she ushered the couple out, assuring them there wouldn't be a problem completing their returns before the fifteenth. She waved them out the door, clutching the handle as it swung closed. Her shoulders rose and fell as she took a deep breath, then she plastered a smile on her face.

"Sorry about the wait. We should be able to get your information sorted out before the next customer arrives." Tara tugged the front of her beige jacket down, then walked around her desk.

"No problem." Ryan slid his foot to change the position of his knee. Boy, the sucker ached today. His mom would say rain was coming. His ibuprofen was wearing off. He dug in his pocket for the pill bottle he hadn't left home without in the months since his injury. "I'm supposed to stay off my feet anyway."

"Knee surgery?" Tara asked as she settled into her seat. Her gaze wandered the desk as if trying to assess where they had left off.

"Torn ACL. I see the surgeon again next week. Then I can get rid of this puppy." He tapped the brace straining the nylon fabric of his pants.

"You said you were staying with your mom, right?"

"Yeah, while I'm on the injured list I can't stay at the track club." He didn't add that the club had released him because they didn't think he would ever recover to competitive shape again. The club physician had claimed his knee was completely shot. But the surgeon had been optimistic, and he clung to that, despite the hesitancy of his physical therapist.

"Yvonne's a good friend of mine. I'm surprised we haven't met before." Tara picked up a pencil and made a note on her calendar.

Ryan knew exactly what she was talking about. His mother's hobbies would keep him on the other side of the country even if his training hadn't. Although if he had known Tara was in her circle of matchmaking prospects, he might have been more open to her suggestions.

The door flew open and an older woman blew in. Almost literally. Her sneakers barely scraped the carpet, and her ivory hair stood on end. "I heard Leslie's in labor and came right from my aerobics class."

Ryan pondered the ability of news to travel so quickly. He hadn't seen Tara make any phone calls. Perhaps the Tenaples had passed on the message.

"Hi, Minnie," Tara said. "They left barely twenty minutes ago. Did Mark call you?"

"No. Beulah Tenaple's senior aerobics class is right after dance aerobics. She said Mark came flying in here like his butt was on fire."

"Leslie had a few contractions, but it is way too early. I'm sure the doctor will get them stopped. I didn't know you were taking aerobics classes."

"It sounded like fun. Gotta keep in shape, you know how it is."

Ryan doubted Minnie and Tara socialized in the same circles, but there wasn't anything wrong with Tara's figure. He appreciated the time and effort it took to keep one's self in good shape.

Minnie's gaze swung to Ryan, and he suddenly wished he had ducked out the door as soon as she came in. She gave him a once-over thorough enough to read the numbers off his credit card through his wind pants. Her evaluation stopped at his left hand and her eyes narrowed.

"And I see you've met this fine young man." She winked at Tara.

Ryan pushed himself to stand and held out his hand. "I'm Ryan. I don't believe we've met."

"Grant, right? Yvonne's son. Your mother and I have been friends since she moved over from Glendale. I heard about your knee. Wasn't there some big race coming up?"

Ryan's stomach churned just thinking about it. He was going to miss it. Again. "The Boston Marathon. It's in four weeks."

"Isn't it the one with the nasty hill everyone cries about?" Minnie smoothed her hair down.

"Heartbreak Hill," Ryan murmured more to himself than to the women. It had broken him last time. This year was supposed to be different. He trained to be a contender, but his body had failed him before he'd set foot on the course.

"Well, your mom enjoys having you around." She clapped her hand on his arm, then squeezed the muscles. "I guess running does something for your arms too." She raised her eyebrows, and Tara shrugged. Minnie reached for her hip. "Shoot. I left my phone at the exercise class. I'm going to make some phone calls. If Leslie's at the hospital, I'll skedaddle. And let you two get back to..." She waved her hand and Ryan wondered what she expected them to get back to besides his tax return. His imagination supplied some ideas, but they weren't on the agenda.

Tara waved as Minnie bounded through the door.

"My mom's friends are so weird," Ryan said when the door whipped shut.

"I think they're a hoot."

"They're something all right." Ryan lowered himself back into his chair. "What else do you need from me?"

Tara had been sorting through his papers and looked up at him. Her lips dropped open. Glossy and red, inviting him in. Their eyes met, and Ryan forgot the rest of the world existed. His mom's friends could sing karaoke naked around them, and he wouldn't have noticed. The only thought in his mind was tasting her lips.

The phone rang and Tara grabbed it. "Knotts Accounting." She made some notes on her calendar, then hung up. "Sorry about that. This time of year is crazy. Maybe we should get your information taken care of before we have another interruption." The alluring facade had disappeared. She turned to her computer and poised her fingers over the keyboard. "How are you filing?"

"Single, no dependents."

A smile tickled the corners of her mouth. Ryan's eyebrows quirked. So she was interested, was she? His time in Carterville might not be as tedious with Tara as a companion. A little fling would help take his mind off his knee and the possible prognosis.

She ran through the rest of the basic questions, then sorted through his papers.

"You have a couple 1099s here, but I don't see any expenses related to them. You can deduct business-related expenses and lower your tax obligation."

"Really? The guy I had do them last year didn't say

anything about it." Ryan straightened in his chair. With his sponsorships dried up, any extra cash would be helpful.

"You may be able to file an amended return. If you're interested, I can look into it, but not until after the fifteenth."

"Cool. What kind of expenses should I have?"

"Anything related to these 1099s. What did you get them for?"

"I have a couple mobile apps that are selling pretty well. The distributors send 1099s for my portion of the sales. I'm working on something that might appeal to college students."

"Okay." Tara tapped her manicured fingertip against her mouse. "Internet service, manuals, professional memberships, graphic artists. You can even deduct part of your rent or mortgage, but that gets more complicated. I can give you a sheet with the specifications."

"Wow. Thanks. That could save me a lot of money. I got nailed last year."

"No problem." She yanked open a drawer and pulled out a checklist. She passed it across the desk to him. He grabbed the edge, tempted to reach closer to her hand to see if her skin was as silky as it appeared.

"You must have been doing this for a while to come up with all that so quickly."

"Actually this is my first year preparing returns." But her face brightened at the compliment. "I've been working with Leslie for three years. I guess I've picked up a few things."

"When will my return be ready?" He wanted to see her again. He wondered if he would need an excuse to see her sooner. She was smart enough to have a decent conversation, but fun enough to keep everything light and easy. He'd be moving back to the training camp after he got the go-ahead from the surgeon. He didn't want to start a serious relationship and be distracted from his recovery and training.

"I'll have it ready for you to review in a couple days. If it's acceptable to you, we can e-file it, and you should have your refund in about two weeks."

"If there is one."

"Well, yeah." She rolled her eyes as if that was obvious. The blue sparkled mischievously.

"Maybe we could go for coffee some time." A couple of days was too long to wait. He had to find someone to spend time with besides his mother.

"I'm free tonight, but for the next few weeks, I'll be tied to my computer."

Chapter Three

Ryan was still figuring out how to maneuver himself out of his vehicle without torquing his knee. Each time he made it out, he was thankful that he'd destroyed his left knee and not his right. If it had been his right, he wouldn't even be driving yet. He was also glad he'd rented an SUV instead of the compact hybrid he'd considered. With a taller vehicle, once he maneuvered his long legs out from under the dashboard, all he had to do was establish his balance and stand up. It didn't require much bending and weight-bearing on his bad knee. Trying to unfold himself from behind the wheel of a small car would be a nightmare of pain.

He prepared himself to stand when a car angled into the slot in the next row. The driver looked like Tara, but he wouldn't have pegged her for driving a nondescript sedan. It couldn't have shocked him any more to see her climb out of a minivan with a passel of kids swarming around her. He'd expect her to drive a convertible or something sporty, not a decades old sedan with an exhaust leak.

She climbed out of the car and slung her purse over her shoulder. She must have switched out her heels because he doubted the lime green gardening clogs had been intended to coordinate with her suit. Her car door creaked menacingly as she slammed it. Looking down at her watch, she muttered something and dashed in his direction.

Ryan stood tentatively and turned to shut his door. Tara looked as good as he remembered. Curvy and vivacious, even with the clogs. He let go of the door, and pivoted on his good leg to reach for the rear door and his crutches. Tara appeared around the back of his vehicle, her head bent, searching in her purse. Before he could call out a greeting, she slammed into him. The next thing he knew he was flat on his back on the pavement with a head of peroxide-blond hair tickling his nose. He coughed as the oxygen that had been slammed from his lungs trickled back in.

The body on top of him squirmed invitingly and lifted away, but she still straddled his legs. He missed the pressure and warmth on his chest immediately. Tara had raised herself to her knees and was shoving her hair away from her face, but her weight shifted to his bad leg and stars swirled in front of his eyes.

"I'm so sorry. I wasn't watching where I was going. I'm running late for a—" She glanced down at his face, then she realized her position and who it was connected to. "To meet you." She scrambled off him and shoved the fabric of her skirt back in place. "I didn't hurt you worse, did I? Let me help you up." She held out her hands.

Ryan blinked, waiting for his personal planetarium to fade. It took a moment to ignore the sensations of Tara's body being pressed against his and evaluate whether any damage had been done. Eventually the stars dissipated, and he was able to take her hands and pull himself onto his good leg. He leaned against his vehicle and brushed off his running pants. "No. I'm fine. No worse than before."

Tara wiped some grit off her pantyhose, but that appeared to be more effort than it was worth. A hole circled her knee and runs raced away from it. She hadn't skinned her knee, but sometimes the road rash appeared later. He knew that from tripping and skidding across the finish line in his last 5k. He checked her other leg to see if there was any damage there. It looked okay. Excellent to be precise.

Tara followed his gaze and saw the mess of her pantyhose. "Drat. My last good pair." She pulled at the fraying nylon and twisted her leg to evaluate the damage. "I'm going to have to ditch these."

Whatever her exercise regimen, it did great things for her gams. He limped around to open the door to his vehicle and remove his crutches. The pads were murder on his armpits, but it felt so much better to get the weight off his leg.

"Shall we?" He tilted his head toward Bart's Sandwich Shop.

She smiled. Lines deepened around her mouth and at the corners of her eyes. "I'd be delighted. I'll duck into the ladies' and ditch the pantyhose."

Ryan watched her thread through the tables to the restroom, trying to suppress the image of her peeling the filmy material down her legs. If his brain kept traveling in this direction, he'd have to contemplate another variety of motions with his bum knee.

She returned before he'd had a chance to peruse the menu. "I hope you don't mind if I grab a sandwich too. I came straight from the office. We had a non-stop stream of customers this afternoon." She settled into the seat across from him. Bart's was hopping with the Friday evening rush. Ryan had secured a two-seater in a corner by the front window as a busboy brushed the remnants of the last diners' meals into a plastic tub.

Local sports memorabilia peppered the walls. Team photos, pennants, game balls and pom-poms all in Carterville Hornet gold and green. Not a hint of the Glendale red and gray, but that was to be expected. Home-town restaurants didn't celebrate the archrivals, even if they were only the next town over.

"It's that time of year, isn't it?"

Tara folded the menu to the burgers. "Yeah and everybody in town heard Leslie has gone into labor. The phone rang constantly. It took me twenty minutes to get through the voice mails. At least a dozen people came in with 1040EZs. Those were a snap to do, but I had to electronically file the extra returns, and the system is always slow on Fridays." Tara shook her head. "I hope Leslie just had a few contractions and can be back to work on Monday. I don't want to be there by myself for the next two weeks. It's too overwhelming."

"I'm sure you'll do fine." He ordered a coffee from the circling waitress. "If you're eating, I think I'll get a sandwich too." The waitress took their orders and left them with a basket of french fries. Ryan took one look at the grease-soaked paper lining and decided to pass. While his training was curtailed, he had to be especially careful about his weight. It would be too easy to add pounds without exercise to burn the calories.

Tara dipped a couple fries in the ranch sauce and popped them in her mouth. "I really shouldn't, but I'm really going to. It will make up for breaking the heel off my shoe when I stepped off the curb."

Ryan laughed. He couldn't help it. "I wondered about the clogs."

Tara slid her foot out to the side of the table. "They don't exactly go with my outfit."

"How'd you end up in Carterville?" Ryan asked. Tara's eyes jerked up to his and he realized it was an abrupt question. He'd been spending too much time with his mother. Asking nosey questions of perfect strangers. Another reason hanging out with Tara would be good for him. He would recover his social graces.

"I moved back about three years ago. Once I'd left, I never imagined I'd come back. I was on to bigger and better things." Her voice trailed off wistfully.

"What did you dream of doing?" Ryan leaned back in his chair. Her story sounded so familiar, except his stay wouldn't be permanent.

Tara faced him, yet she stared over his shoulder. "I was steps away from being a cheerleader in the NFL."

Ryan started. A professional cheerleader? Perhaps Tara was out of his league. Cheerleaders barely gave him a second glance. They only had eyes for the football or basketball team, not the track team.

"I made it through the first round of auditions, and the coach and choreographer were encouraging. I thought I had it in the bag. Then they showed us the new uniforms."

To Ryan's eye, any outfit from dental floss to a garbage bag would have been drool-inducing on Tara. Though her current coordinating suit and jacket disguised her figure, it would be impossible to dismiss the curves underneath it. While the blouse was conservatively cut, it wasn't prudish by any means. "I don't see how that would be a problem."

"They wanted perfection and I have some scars the skimpier uniforms wouldn't cover. I don't care if people see them, but it's so frustrating to have a little wrinkled skin ruin my career. They said I could try out again the following year, if I had plastic surgery to fix the scars, but I had enough surgeries after the car accident."

He shook his head. He knew exactly what it felt like to not be able to do what you wanted to do.

She pounded her fist against the table. "I had that audition in the bag, even if I was the oldest one there."

"You seem to be doing well here though. Maybe it was a good change."

Tara tipped her head from side to side, evaluating his words. "Leslie keeps things simple for me, so I can handle it."

"You don't give yourself enough credit." He knew it sounded quaint, but something told him Tara had more to share with the world than being an adolescent boy's fantasy. She had known more about what his tax return needed than his previous preparer, and he'd been in business for twenty years.

"That's sweet, but..." She shook her head. "I'm aware of my limitations. What about you? I showed you mine. Now you have to show me yours."

Ryan arched an eyebrow. "I didn't exactly see your scars."

"Not exactly appropriate for a first date." Her eyes twinkled.

"Should I ask for a second one now?" Ryan's imagination was in overdrive picturing where Tara's scars might be. He reached for the zipper on the ankle of his running pants. He unzipped the opening and rolled his pant leg up to reach the brace that encased his knee. The metal bands and hinges that stabilized his knee were padded with an absorbent terry cloth, but it still left red indentations on his skin. "I'm supposed to be walking with a cane by now." He prodded the strained, purple skin of his incisions.

"What happened?"

He pushed his pant leg down to his ankle and slipped the zipper back in place. "Marathon runners usually succumb to repetitive use injuries, but I tripped over a root on a trail run. Twisted my knee. Haven't run a step since."

"I'm so sorry." She reached across the table and touched the back of his hand. Sparks shot through his skin. When she didn't move her hand away, he wrapped his hand around hers. "It must be devastating."

"I hope the surgeon can explain why my recovery is taking so long. I should be running by now." With Tara's hand in his, his plight didn't seem so desperate. "I'll be able to run again soon. My physical therapist isn't as optimistic, but the surgeon will know what isn't healing."

"I hope so. I couldn't imagine not being able to do something I loved so much. I can still do dance routines. Not in front of thousands of screaming fans, but not being able to do it at all..." Her blue eyes lit with excitement and Ryan found himself mesmerized by the little green flecks. The roaring in his ears was as loud as an arena.

He could see Tara with her blonde hair bouncing and those little sparkly pom-poms shaking. He shook his head to dismiss the image before the fantasy took over more than his thoughts.

"Yeah. The other doctors told me I would never run again, but it doesn't make sense. I could understand if it was a repetitive use injury where something wore out, but I fell. It was a split second. Broken bones heal. I'll be back to normal soon. One little stumble can't change the course of my life."

Chapter Four

One stumble, one second, one dumb decision had affected her career. If she hadn't fought with that guy over the rum bottle after graduation, she would still be cheerleading. She wouldn't have melted skin across her abdomen and she probably wouldn't have needed breast implants.

Tara wouldn't consider surgery to change her body now, but only because she had been through all those skin grafts. Who knew what she would have decided without those procedures?

Their food arrived and Tara reluctantly let go of Ryan's hand to flatten her napkin across her lap. Ryan asked for extra carrots with his sandwich. She wished she could be that disciplined. Before she could swirl her potato wedges in ranch dressing, her cell phone drummed out her favorite girl power song. She dropped the wedge and wiped her hands on her napkin. "I'm sorry, I should have put it on silent." She reached into her purse to send the noisy interruption to voice mail. "Oh, it's Mark. I should take this."

Ryan nodded and dug into his sandwich.

"How are you holding up?" she asked after greeting

Mark.

"Hanging in there. Trying to keep Leslie calm."

"What's going on? Is she in labor? Did they get the contractions stopped?" Tara was peppering Mark with questions, but they were flying out of her mouth before she could stop them.

"I'm not sure where to start." Mark half-laughed. "Slow down. She was in labor, but they were able to stop the contractions. For now."

"For now? What does that mean? Is she going to have the baby soon?" Tara's mental calendar popped up. The baby wasn't due for eight more weeks. While she didn't know a lot about pregnancy, she knew babies weren't supposed to come that early. Could the baby even survive? She pressed the phone closer to her ear so she could hear over the din in the restaurant.

"The doctor said as soon as she starts moving around again, the contractions will pick back up. They recommend Leslie stay off her feet and rest for at least a week."

"A week?" Tara managed to squeak out. Her stomach swam. A week? She'd expected the weekend, but five business days? Their busiest days, too. Oh dear. She couldn't hold the office together for a week without Leslie.

Ryan's gaze jerked from the window, and he arched his eyebrow in question. Tara mouthed, "Not good."

Mark said in her ear, "She's been trying to get things ready for you between the tests and such. Trying to make lists, things to remind you, but every time she thought of something her heart rate would jump and the doctor freaked. He grabbed her smart phone away from her. I thought he was going to toss it in the garbage."

"If he had, Leslie probably would have had the baby right then." Tara tried for a laugh, but it did little to mask her terror at the enormity of the situation. A premature baby for her friends, and their livelihood resting on her slumping shoulders. She had to stop feeling sorry for herself. Their concerns were much greater than hers. "Will she and the baby be all right?"

She heard Mark's deep breath through the phone. He was struggling to be strong, too. "The doctors are monitoring everyone closely. If anything changes in a way they don't like, they will intercede. I promised to keep her phone away from her, so if you have questions, call me. But, for the most part, you're going to be on your own."

The french fries squirmed in her stomach. Her sandwich would have been a horrid knot. As it was, she wouldn't have been surprised if the fries had metamorphosed into wriggling tadpoles. *On her own?* "Mark. I can't do this alone. Leslie handled all the complicated stuff. Who are we going to get to do that?" Hysteria edged her voice and she tried to push it away. Her best friends were dealing with life and death, and she was whining about taxes. She had to pull herself together, but the strings were snapping faster than she could grab them. She didn't dare meet Ryan's eyes. He probably thought she was a whiny wimp. "Is there anyone to help?"

"There was someone scheduled to come after the baby was born. What was her name?"

"She couldn't come until after tax season. We will need someone right away."

"I'll call you later with a name, but right now I need you to reassure Leslie you can do this. She believes you can, but it would do her a lot of good to hear you say it."

Tara wanted to throw a two-year-old temper tantrum. She couldn't do this. But she'd try her hardest for Leslie. Leslie had done so much for her. It was the weekend. They were only open to customers for half a day on Saturday so they could catch up on the work. She'd have some quiet time to muddle through what she could. Monday was forty-eight hours away. She'd worry about it later.

Leslie's voice came over the phone. "If I remember

correctly — I was looking at the schedule before Mark took my phone." Tara was glad she was across town from the daggers Leslie had to be shooting in Mark's direction. "Tomorrow and Monday are repeat customers. If you have any trouble, you can look at the returns from last year."

Hoping the tone of her voice was believable, Tara replied, "Maybe Minnie can help with the phones. Everything will be just fine. You relax and keep that baby baking for as long as possible."

Tara hoped God would forgive her little white lie. She could survive two days. Just because she was learning this by the sink or swim method, she couldn't ruin the business in less than a week. Could she?

"You're a better woman than I am, if you can put up with Minnie for that long. You know how she gossips. Don't forget your college applications are due on the sixteenth."

Tara bit her tongue. She *had* forgotten. How was she going to finish those essays while working around the clock? She'd never get into the accounting program. Why set herself up for failure? She knew she wasn't college material.

Leslie said goodbye and Mark returned to the phone. "Thanks, Tara. It will help her to relax to know you've got things covered. I better go. The doctor is here. Oh, she says if you need help to call Charlie on Monday." Mark disconnected.

Off the top of her head, Tara couldn't remember a Charlie, but she was sure the necessary information was in Leslie's computer. She'd look it up tomorrow.

"What's going on?" Ryan asked as Tara dropped the phone back into her purse.

Tara pushed her uneaten burger away. Her stomach was churning too much to contemplate adding the grilled beef to the mix. She explained everything Mark had said, ending with, "I'm terrified about this. The baby's too early and there's too much at the office only Leslie handles."

Ryan reached for her hand again. "You'll call Charlie and

do what you can until he arrives. You can make it."

The strength in his hand flowed into hers. Tara attempted a smile she didn't feel. She doubted it would be easy.

Chapter Five

Moving in with his mother hadn't been as awful as Ryan had expected. He'd been home almost six days and hadn't felt the urge to flee yet.

However, when the doorbell rang five minutes earlier, Ryan's fight or flight instinct kicked into overdrive. His mom's friends crowded the doorway. The Ladies Night Out they called themselves. As soon as he opened the door, they exclaimed about how handsome he was, how thin he'd grown, and how long he'd been on crutches. A cacophony of clucking hens. And his ears were ringing.

"Ryan, you are just skin and bones." Someone pinched his cheek. He tried to inch away, but another woman slipped her arm through his. A feat considering his crutches, but it also eliminated his escape. He recognized her as the one who was friends with Tara. What was her name? Minnie?

"Do you have a girlfriend?" she asked. He couldn't shake her off without losing his balance.

Another one bustled in. "How long are you home for?"

There was nowhere to go. They had him cornered in the entryway and attacked from every side. He felt like the

29

squirrel he'd seen on his last run. A pair of birds had dive-bombed it and herded it away when it scurried too close to their nest. Although instead of an intruder being chased away, he was pretty sure he was the prey.

"Why are you on crutches?" He tried to back away, but put weight on his bad knee and his leg crumpled. The pain shot up to his hip and exploded fireworks behind his eyes. He swayed and slammed into the wall, knocking the air out of his lungs. If the women had been hovering before, they swarmed now. He couldn't regain his feet or his breath as they all grabbed for his arms and crutches. The crutches disappeared from view as the hands clutched, twisted, and grabbed. He slid down the wall until he sat on the floor, wondering if survival was possible. No way he could stand up until the mob dispersed. In all the hysteria, someone else pinched his behind. Certainly not by accident.

That was it. He was getting out of here. He resisted the urge to swat at their fluttering hands, but he couldn't flee unless they backed away. There was no way he could stand without knocking someone else down. Despite the condition of his knee, he feared for the elderly hips and arthritic bones.

Luckily, his mother swooped in before he curled into a fetal position and let them bat him around like grizzly bears with their lunch. The Ladies hovered as his mom helped him to his feet and retrieved his crutches. He propped them under his arms and allowed the panic to recede. Then she dispersed The Ladies into the dining room where the table was laden with trays of carrots, celery, broccoli florets, sports drinks, and bottled water.

"Carrot sticks!" the lady in pink exclaimed.

"What do you think we are, rabbits?" from the one in red.

"If we are serious about this project, it isn't a choice," Minnie said. "We've all got a lot of work to do."

The looks of disgust lessened, but didn't disappear. From what he remembered, the Ladies Night Out usually feasted on spiked punch and other decadent treats. The Ladies picked up the luncheon trays and filled them with vegetables.

"Can I fill you a tray?" one of the Ladies asked. She wore a blue sweat suit with something embroidered across the behind. He wasn't brave enough to read what it said.

"No thanks. I already ate." He patted his stomach to emphasize how full he was.

She arched an eyebrow. "Suit yourself. An extra meal wouldn't hurt." She studied his marathon runner frame for a moment, then tilted her head toward a woman in a matching sweat suit. "He might be just the thing."

Minnie pursed her lips. "Maybe. But you know what Yvonne said. He's not staying."

"Right." The woman in blue bit into a celery stick. "It's too bad."

Ryan wasn't sure what they were talking about, but he had a good idea. He wasn't going to commit to Carterville, let alone any woman in it. He didn't dare ask any questions, in case that implied acquiescence to whatever they were scheming. No matter what their plot was, he didn't want any part of it.

He was at his mom's to heal, get back to running and racing again, no matter what the doctor said. They had been wrong before. He would miss the Boston Marathon this year, but he would be ready to conquer it next year.

"I thought you guys met on Fridays." He tucked the crutches under his arms and hobbled into the kitchen after his mother and as far from her friends as he could get. If he'd known they would be descending on his mom's living room at noon, he would have made himself scarce for the whole day. Checking in on Tara was sounding better and better, but he didn't want to interrupt her at work. He knew she would be having a stressful morning, and he didn't want to disturb her concentration.

"Usually." Mom emptied a tray of ice into a bowl. "We're

working on a special project and we need to do aerobics. Hey, maybe you could show us some stretches?"

Aerobics? If the crowd of women that had overrun him hadn't been wearing more spandex than age-appropriate, he would have been shocked. His mother considered walking to the refrigerator during the commercials of her soap operas 'quite enough exercise, thank you very much.' A quick glance into the dining room confirmed her friends shared that philosophy.

Maybe that was the simple reason for the aerobics. They had decided to get in better shape. Adopt a healthier lifestyle. Good for them.

"Heck, no." His heart was still pumping as if he'd just finished a sprint workout on the track. "I'm not spending another minute with those raptors."

He packed his crutches and his laptop and headed for the library to figure out the bugs in the mobile recording app he'd written.

Chapter Six

Tara locked the front door behind Minnie and closed her eyes. As much as she loved Minnie, she didn't know if working with her was the best option for getting through the days without Leslie. When Minnie wasn't answering phones, she was dishing out the latest gossip. While all of it couldn't be true — in fact, Tara was pretty sure Minnie stitched it up out of whole cloth— it was entertaining, and unfortunately, distracting. During one of Minnie's longer phone calls, Tara had managed to dash off an email to the only Charles in Leslie's address book. No Charlie appeared, so this contact must have been who Leslie was referring to.

After e-filing all the day's returns she could complete, Tara locked the office and headed home shortly after five to change. Not bad for a Saturday. She had to admit she liked the professional image of her business suit, but it always felt good to slip into sweats at the end of the day. Tara hung her suit in her closet and pulled on a pair of mint green sweatpants with a matching hoodie. She pulled the pins out of her French twist and wound her hair into a messy bun. After sliding her feet into her tennis shoes, she grabbed her notebook and prepared to camp out at the library with her admissions essays until it closed.

The deadlines for turning in her applications were rapidly approaching. She would have to decide soon if she should get her accounting degree. Leslie had been encouraging her and had even offered to help pay for classes, but Tara wasn't sure she was cut out for all the complicated regulations. No one else had trusted her with that kind of responsibility.

When she arrived at the library, she headed up to the librarian's desk. Lisa, her favorite reference librarian, saw her approaching and pulled a manila file from her drawer. "I didn't expect you in today. How's Leslie?"

"I haven't gotten an update from Mark yet today, but she's on bed rest for a week."

Lisa put her hand over her chest. "Oh no. Only a week? That's surprising. Once you're on bed rest, you are usually stuck there until the baby is born."

"I can't contemplate Leslie being gone for this week, let alone any more than the next two." Tara sighed. "I am going to need a hazelnut coffee."

"Essay time, huh?" She handed Tara the folder. "Here are some samples and the admissions information for the other programs Leslie recommended."

Tara opened the folder and shook her head at the first brochure. "Forensic Accounting? I don't even know what that is." She slid the folder in her notebook. "I don't know why she thinks I can do this. I'm a cheerleader in every stereotype of the word."

Lisa laughed. "Leslie said you flew through the tax preparation classes like no one else. She has a lot of faith in you."

"After the next few days, we'll know for sure if it's warranted. Do you have a quiet place I can work on this stuff?"

"I'd sneak you into the conference room, but the heat is out again. You'd turn into a frozen treat in an hour. This place is falling apart. Minnie says she has a plan to raise funds for the renovation. We could use them. There's one study room that doesn't have a drafty window."

"Does it come with a masseuse?" Tara rolled her shoulders and let her head loll to the side.

"If it did, honey, you'd never see me at the reference desk."

Tara's lips curved up. "What do you have to stress about? Everything is perfectly calm at the library."

Lisa snorted. "Yeah, by the time you get here. All the teens with no place to go after school have been picked up by their parents or the police." Lisa's phone rang. "I'll have the last room open for you by the time you get your coffee."

"Thanks." Tara headed down to the coffee bar and ordered her hazelnut coffee. "I'm going to splurge and get whipped cream on top."

"Coming right up." The teenage girl with the paper hat behind the counter scribbled something on a paper cup and moved toward the coffee machine with all the speed of a hibernating beaver.

I hope my coffee's still hot by the time she gets it to me. Tara leaned against the bar and waited.

"Funny meeting you here." Ryan appeared at her side. She'd been staring at the display of coffee beans and wondering if she had anything intelligent to write in her admissions essay, so she hadn't heard his crutches creak.

"We keep running into each other." She grinned. Maybe things were looking up. She smoothed her hair. "At least I didn't cream you this time. You didn't hurt your leg any worse last time, did you?"

He was wearing wind pants and a T-shirt for the Chicago Marathon. He looked comfortable despite being propped on crutches. Like popcorn and a good movie. Something she hadn't enjoyed in a long time.

"No, it couldn't get any worse." His face sobered.

Minnie couldn't have been right. "You really have to have your leg amputated? You said surgery, but I thought an amputation was gossip."

"Amputated?" Ryan laughed so hard he almost fell off his crutches. "What? No, who told you that?" he managed to reply between snorts.

Great. He thinks I'm an idiot for believing it. Oh well, him and every other nice guy. It shouldn't matter anyway. "Minnie mentioned it. I didn't think it was true. You know how gossip gets the story all out of whack."

Ryan chuckled. "My mom's pretty good at mangling things. Anything else I should know about?"

"Undercover work?"

Ryan made a confused face. "Like police work?" When Tara nodded, he said, "No, but if I was, I couldn't tell you."

Tara laughed. "That's what I told Minnie. Shacking up with a politician's wife?" She pulled a loose tendril of hair from the end of her bun and twisted it around her finger.

"Wow. Whose?" He scratched the back of his ear while leaning on one crutch. "Maybe I should."

"I guess if you have to ask, that one isn't true either." Tara winked.

The lines around Ryan's mouth deepened when he laughed. Tara wanted to run her finger along them. She jammed her hand into her pocket. While Ryan seemed like a great guy, she would be working around the clock for the next two weeks. No time for a few dates, and Ryan would return to his training after he saw the specialist. Her disappointment must have shown on her face.

"Sorry if I'm not as exciting as the gossip."

"I've been around long enough to know how much of the gossip to trust." She winked again.

Ryan nodded and moved to fill his coffee cup from the

free coffee carafe. The cup wobbled as he tried to balance on his crutches and work the spigot on the coffee pot.

"Let me help." Tara took the cup. Her fingers brushed against his and warmth shot through her. Luckily the cup was empty or she would have sloshed hot coffee over both their hands.

"Thanks. Anterior cruciate ligament sounds a little like amputation."

"Only because they both start with 'a'." Tara let the warm brew gurgle into his cup. Just as she finished, the barista brought Tara's coffee with its gigantic swirl of whipped cream. The drink looked awfully frothy next to his sober black one. She started to hand him his cup, then realizing how awkward it would be to carry hot coffee while on crutches, she said, "Let me bring this to your seat. It's the least I can do after knocking you over."

Ryan grinned and dimples formed in his cheeks. Some of Tara's stress slipped away. "I'd appreciate it. I'm camped over this way."

Tara grabbed a couple of napkins then followed him.

"How'd your morning go?" Ryan asked as he navigated to a short set of stairs.

"Busy, busy, but Minnie — you met her yesterday — came in to help answer the phone. And I found the contact information for the person Leslie suggested. There's a ramp over there." Tara inclined her head around a bookcase.

"This is shorter." He moved the crutches to one hand and hopped up the five stairs on his right foot. "Sounds like things are going smoothly then."

"Well, I haven't heard back from Charlie yet, but yes, so far." She pushed away the threatening queasiness. "One day at a time."

"That's all you can do." Ryan turned toward a desk along the windows. A laptop, headphones, and backpack littered the table. A fleece pullover was draped over the back of the chair.

Tara placed his coffee next to the computer. She started to go, but Ryan said, "Do you know anything about a project my mom and her friends may be working on?"

Tara thought for a minute, then shrugged. "Other than fundraising for the library's building project, I don't know. They say I'm not old enough to be a member of their group. Unless..." She tapped her lip with her finger. "They do owe me a favor."

"Would it include carrot sticks and aerobics?" Ryan asked as he settled in his seat and slid his crutches under the desk.

"I don't think so, but I wouldn't question their particular brand of magic."

"So what brings you here? I'd think you'd want to veg out in front of the TV during your down time."

Tara winced. Why was she even contemplating college when she'd never be taken seriously? "Leslie wants me to take some accounting courses this fall, and I need to finish my applications."

"Good for you. I think it would be hard to go back to college after having been out for a while."

"It's even harder if you never went in the first place. I didn't need a college degree to be on the dance squad, and I don't know what to write for these essays. I haven't written more than an email in years."

"Find something you are passionate about."

"Writing essays doesn't make the list." Tara grimaced.

"If you wanted to answer phones for the rest of your life, you wouldn't have taken the tax prep classes."

"I took those to help Leslie." She was flattered Ryan remembered the detail though.

"From what I've heard, you sailed through them. You must have some ability in this area."

"Did you hear that from the same gossip that said you were donating your amputated leg to a politician's wife?"

He laughed. "Sometimes they do get it right."

She shook her head, blinking at the flickering fluorescent light above her head. "I do like how neatly everything comes together. But I'm so scared I'll screw something up. This is people's money we're talking about. Lots of people depend on their refunds."

"You'll practice. It's what school is about — making mistakes, so you do it right when it matters."

"So I write my essay about screwing up?" Tara blew on the edge of her coffee before taking a sip.

"And what you learned from it."

"Well, that makes sense." In theory. She could make mistakes with the best — or should it be worst? — of them, but she still didn't have a topic.

Chapter Seven

"Charles Silverman." He winked and flashed a capped smile. "But you can call me Charles."

"Nice to meet you, Charles." Tara held the door open and allowed him to pass through before locking it behind him. She hadn't expected to hear from him until after lunch today, and he'd shown up an hour before the office opened. She held out her hand. "I'm Tara Mansfield."

His spring trench coat protected a swanky suit that, by her guess, was at least two years old. The current fashion had a wider lapel and three buttons on the jacket instead of four. Charles didn't seem like the type of guy to wear an out of fashion suit but maybe he was a little down on his luck and Leslie was trying to help him out. It would explain his ability to be here at a moment's notice. "I'm glad you were able to come so quickly. I hope we didn't make you leave anyone in the lurch at your current office."

Charles was still holding her hand. She wriggled it free and resisted the urge to wipe it on her suit skirt. His skin had an oily sheen to match his slicked hair. He was probably around Leslie's age, a couple years older than herself, but he looked like he'd lived hard.

"Not a problem, babe. I'm currently between positions and this will be a great way to kill some time." He gave her an appraising look she remembered from her cheerleading days. *What did he estimate her retail value to be?* If he thought he would get anywhere with her, she had a can of pepper spray in her purse she'd introduce him to. While she knew she couldn't survive the week without his help, she was capable of handling her day-to-day duties, despite his evaluation of her physical attributes.

And she despised being called 'babe.' It usually meant that the guys were too lazy to learn her name.

"Let me give you a tour. Show you the coat closet, the office, the break room and such." She waved him around her desk and toward the back hallway.

"Bathroom's here. A closet there." She pointed to doors as they passed. "This is the break room." She pushed open the door at the end of the hall. Charles stepped around her and into the room.

"Hmm. A futon? What services do you provide there?" He slid a leering look her way.

Ewww. Leslie had suggested this guy? No wonder he was between positions. She hated to think about what he actually meant. What a creep.

"I don't know what kind of offices you've worked in, Mr. Silverman, but we handle finances here and that is it. Leslie took naps on the futon because she was pregnant."

"Oh yeah." The words came out dry, like he didn't actually believe her.

Another reason to hope Leslie would get out of bed rest, and be able to return to work.

"So where's my office?" Charles asked, heading back toward the reception area. He stopped in front of Leslie's door. "Here?"

Tara hadn't had a chance to think about where he would

work, but the idea of having a door between them had appeal. There was space for another desk in the reception area, and she and Leslie had discussed how they would arrange things when they were able to hire another person. She supposed he'd have to work in Leslie's office. It didn't seem right for him to take over Leslie's space, but she couldn't have him greeting customers either. It would only be for a few days, she reminded herself as she opened the door for him.

"This is Leslie's office. I haven't had a chance to organize things for you yet." As she said it she realized how inane she sounded. Files were stacked neatly in the inbox and outbox bins on the desk. The blotter, phone, and clock were all square with the edges of the desk. The only hint that anyone had worked here in the last month was the open file on the blotter with a pen on top of it and the chair turned away from the desk. Exactly as Tara had left it Friday afternoon.

"Same old Leslie, not a hair out of place. Does she still wear the French twists so tight her eyes bug out?" Charles wandered around the desk and picked up the photo of Mark from its place of honor next to her computer screen. He laughed and slapped it face down.

Tara stood in the doorway, desperately itching to return Mark's picture to its proper standing.

"It's not as bad as I expected." Charles dropped his briefcase in the middle of Leslie's desk and shrugged his coat off his shoulders. "It'll do, for now."

"Okay." Tara stood in the doorway wondering what she should do next. Take his coat? Offer him coffee? Leslie never asked her to do any of these things, but she was acting as the hostess here. "We don't open for another half hour, so make yourself comfortable."

"Great." Charles held his coat out to Tara.

She took it as if it was a bag of dirty diapers. "I'll hang this up." She turned toward the door. "I'll get the file for your first appointment. You'll have a chance to skim it before they arrive."

"Send them in. I'll have a coffee with two sugars and half a teaspoon of cream."

"I don't think we have any cream. Is non-dairy creamer all right?" She could guess his answer. A big fat no.

"Skimping on the coffee supplies? Things must be tight. I knew Leslie couldn't get this place off the ground."

Charles hadn't had one nice thing to say about Leslie since he arrived. Tara couldn't believe Leslie had recommended him. He didn't seem like the type of person she would associate with.

"Leslie and I both drink our coffee black during the day. We used to keep cream for the customers, but it usually spoiled before it was used so we stopped buying it."

The phone on Tara's desk rang.

"You better get that. It looks like Leslie can't afford to lose customers." Charles pressed the power button on the computer.

Tara hid her scowl and headed for the door, anxious for any excuse to leave Charles's presence. His evaluations of the office were annoying at the least, since the entire place had been renovated from top to bottom in the last three years. She grabbed the handset on her desk and tucked the receiver between her ear and shoulder.

"Knotts Accounting. How may I help you?" She draped Charles's coat over the back of her chair.

"It's a boy!" the voice exclaimed. She recognized Mark immediately.

"What? Leslie had the baby? Is everyone okay?" She stopped her questions before she asked when Leslie would be back to work. With a new baby, she'd be out beyond the end of tax season. She grabbed Charles's coat off her chair and hung it in the closet. She didn't need to be in front of her computer for this call. She closed the closet door and headed for the coffee pot in the break room.

"Everyone's okay. The baby's still baking. We saw something unmistakable on the ultrasound though." Mark laughed.

"Congratulations on the boy. How exciting! When can Leslie come home?" She poured a cup of coffee and dumped the required two sugars into a mug with their logo on it. Charles never suggested a replacement for his half tablespoon of cream so Tara didn't worry about it.

"They are keeping her in the hospital a little longer. Her blood pressure isn't coming down. The radiology tech saw something on the ultrasound she was concerned about too. We're waiting to hear more from Leslie's doctor."

"I hoped she'd be able to come home."

"Me, too. At least she's getting rest here. She's not allowed to be on her feet for more than five minutes at a time. Hold on a sec." Mark said something muffled, then came back to her. "She wants to know how you are holding up."

"Tell her I'm doing fine. No need to worry." Tara hoped her uneasiness wasn't evident in her voice. She placed Charles's coffee in front of him, then returned to her desk. "The person she suggested is here already. That should help. He seems eager to get to work."

He had certainly powered up the computer quickly. Maybe the bad vibes she was getting from him were simply from years of working with men who only appreciated women for their bodies.

"Great. She'll be relieved. Hopefully it will help her relax. She's been so upset about dumping all this on you."

"She's got better things to worry about than me." Tara's confidence wavered. Leslie knew she couldn't handle this and it was making her condition worse. Tara couldn't let her fears affect Leslie and Mark's baby. She had to handle this. Do whatever was necessary to keep the office running. She'd work around the clock to prove herself to Leslie.

"Tara!" an irritated voice called from Leslie's office.

"I better go. Tell Leslie to take it easy and keep that baby baking as long as possible." She tried to shake away the uneasiness. Leslie was depending on her.

"Will do. I'll talk to you later."

Tara hung up and went to see what Charles needed. If it was about his coffee, he would have to learn to doctor it himself. She leaned through the doorway. "Yes?"

"Could you log me onto the computer system?"

"Sure." Tara started toward the desk, then stopped. "Actually why don't I create a login for you? Then you can set everything up the way you want."

Charles hesitated. "Will I still be able to access the client files?"

"Yes. Just not Leslie's private files."

He didn't look altogether happy, but something about him made Tara want to be cautious. She backed away from the desk. "Is there anything else?"

"I want my password to be 'big kahuna.'"

"We use a password generator and change the passwords on all logins every two weeks. We are very concerned about our system and our clients' privacy."

Charles grunted, and Tara took that as agreement. She returned to her desk and set up the system login and password for Charles. She jotted down the alphanumeric code on a sticky note as Dinah and Fred arrived with their sniffly grandson, Bryson Paul. Everyone called him Boppy. Much of Carterville had hoped the unfortunate nickname would fade before he reached school age, but it stuck like the peanut butter smeared on the side of his mouth.

"Hi. Have a seat. I'll be right back." Tara pulled the paper off the pad and brought it to Charles. He grumbled about the complicated code. Tara rolled her eyes.

"The Halloways are here. Their return is done, so I only have to go over it with them. You can get yourself settled."

Dinah was unwinding a scarf from Boppy's neck as he

sneezed three times in succession. After each sneeze, Dinah blessed him. Fred pulled a red handkerchief from his rear jeans pocket and swished it across Boppy's face.

"Grandpa." Boppy giggled between sniffs.

"Hello Tara. We didn't mean to be late. Judi called and asked us to pick up Boppy. She couldn't send him to preschool today because of his cold, and she had an appointment in Glendale this morning."

"No problem. It shouldn't take long to go over your return." Tara eased into a routine she had performed many times. That was all she needed to do right now. Her job. "Boppy can play with the toys." The dark-haired boy had already spied the toy box and wiggled out of Fred's grasp. Fred let him go, and Boppy dug through the toys. He sorted out the Matchbox cars and flung them around the floor screaming, "Are there more?" after each one.

Dinah stood and directed him to pick up the cars. He retrieved them and dropped them on the play table.

Tara eased the Halloways' file from the stack on her desk. She handed them a copy of their return and explained the numbers and the bottom line. As she spoke, Boppy's play sounds grew louder. The cars were having a high speed chase around the office floor complete with screeching brakes, police sirens, and gunfire. Dinah and Fred admonished him to keep it down, but the gunfire grew to machine guns and dive bombers. He was loud but not disruptive to Tara's conversation.

"What is going on out here?" Charles stood in the office doorway. He glared at the boy as if he'd never seen a small child before.

Tara spun on her chair. "This is Fred and Dinah Halloway. I'm reviewing their personal tax return. They are part owners of Halloways' Tractor Repair and Halloways' Custom Hot Rods."

Charles grimaced, but Tara thought it might have been an

attempt at a smile. Even if he wouldn't be here for long, it would help him to do his job to know who the movers and shakers in Carterville were. "Tara, can I speak with you for a second?"

"Sure." Tara excused herself to the Halloways and followed Charles into Leslie's office.

"Why's the kid here?" Charles asked as soon as she was in the office and he had shut the door.

"His grandparents are watching him while his mother is at a meeting." She crossed her arms over her chest and his gaze shifted downward.

"Did they have to take him along? This is no place for a kid."

She tipped her head, so he had to look in her eyes again. "They can't very well leave a five-year-old home alone."

"Can't he sit quietly while you finish up? Kids are supposed to be seen and not heard. I'd prefer not seen as well."

"We have the toys so children can play while their parents have their taxes done. We have drawn several new clients because the parents don't have to arrange for and pay a babysitter."

"Ridiculous. No wonder Leslie needs help here." Charles rolled his eyes.

Enough with the digs at Leslie already. Why was he here if he thought so little of her?

"Leslie's doing fine. Most children we barely notice. Boppy would be noisy even if he was sleeping."

Charles shrugged. He waved his hand as if everything around him was ridiculous. "Whatever. I'll keep my door closed until they leave."

Okay, Tara mouthed to herself as she walked back to her desk. Obviously wherever Charles normally worked, it wasn't with the general public. Maybe he only had corporate clients in the big city. She settled in her seat and picked up where she left off with the Halloways. She'd have to cut him some slack. It would take him a day or two to get used to how they did things here.

Fred signed the bottom of his return, then handed Dinah the paper and pen to sign on her line.

"How's Leslie doing?" Dinah passed the paper back to Tara.

"She's going to be in the hospital for a few days yet." Tara tilted her head toward Leslie's office. "Charles has agreed to help us out while she is out of commission."

"Oh." Dinah made a face, then whispered, "You couldn't find anyone else? He's not very personable."

Tara sighed. "He arrived this morning. I think he'll come around. We do things a bit differently than he's used to." She hoped he would. This beginning wasn't promising.

"Maybe he won't be so uptight after he warms up." Dinah stood and pulled on her coat. "We better go. Fred needs to get back to the shop."

As Fred rounded up Boppy, Charles stepped out of his office and stood next to Tara's desk. He scowled at the little boy as he picked up the cars and pitched them into the toy box with explosions as they landed. As Fred and Boppy walked passed him, Boppy sneezed, leaving a sprayed arc across Charles' pants.

"Have a nice day." The Halloways waved and left.

Charles looked down at his pinstriped trousers in disgust. "I assume there is anti-bacterial spray around here somewhere."

Tara hid her evil grin behind a tax form. "In the break room under the sink."

"If any more kids come in, I'm leaving." He slapped the folder on her desk.

Tara was tempted to say, "Don't let the door hit you on the way out," but she needed his help and she couldn't afford to have him walk out. He'd barely been here an hour, and she'd already had to bite her tongue a half-dozen times. This did not bode well for the next two weeks.

"I'll make sure they stay in the play area." Most kids did anyway. Boppy's visit was actually pretty quiet. For him. When his parents, Bryce and Judi, had come in, he had run up and down the hall singing nursery rhymes until Bryce caught him and held him in a straight jacket hold until he fell asleep. Between snores bits of the nursery rhymes popped out. After that visit, Tara had learned not to offer him a cookie until they were about to leave. Boppy's little sister had been entirely pleasant, but she was only four months old and couldn't get into much trouble yet.

"Any other weird practices you have here I should know about? Do people hitch their horses up outside? Roll up the sidewalks at night?"

Tara decided to ignore the last comments, figuring he was grumpy because he had gotten up so early. She picked up a stack of files on her desk. "Here are the rest of the client files for today. And this is the schedule. I've starred the ones I can take care of."

"You're giving me orders?" Charles shook the files at her. "Who's the CPA here?"

This guy was pulling rank on her? What was his deal? He agreed to come here, and now he was acting like it was a huge inconvenience to actually do the work.

"We can tear up the contract any time. You are free to walk out of here."

As soon as she said the words, she wished she could snatch them back. What if he did leave? Who was left to call? She knew Leslie well enough to know she wouldn't have recommended him if there was anyone else. Charles was the rock bottom.

Charles shook his head. "No. No. I'll stay. I don't want you telling me what to do. If you want me to help you, you need to let me work the way I need to work."

Tara sighed. "I can't do anything about people bringing their children with them. It's a service we advertise. We can't change it now. Anything else, you let me know what you need and I'll do my best." She hated how appeasing that sounded.

Charles's gaze slid to the front of her blouse. He tucked the folders under his arm. "You could start by getting me some cream for my coffee."

Tara glanced at her watch. They had an appointment in five minutes. She could make it to the grocery store and back... If she could find an open cashier. Not likely on senior day. "Sure thing. I'll be right back. The Winstons usually arrive early, so I'll be back as soon as I can. Is there anything else?"

"Some donuts. Not those plain ones, something with filling and sprinkles."

Tara grabbed her keys from her desk drawer and dashed out the door, wondering if having Charles around would ease her workload or increase it.

Chapter Eight

Tara checked her calendar. Fourteen more days of tax season. Then she could breathe again. Charles would be out of her hair. She could survive a few more days. She might turn into a walking zombie but at least she'd be alive. Or was it undead? Undead would certainly describe her current state. The bags under her eyes already required a thick coating of concealer to hide the purple. She could use some cucumber slices to reduce the puffiness, but she didn't have time to keep her eyes closed.

She sipped her coffee, hoping for a jolt from the caffeine. The double shot espresso didn't have the punch it used to. She might need to bump up to a triple for the next two weeks.

"Tara!" Charles called.

She also needed to hide her letter opener. The one with the long, shiny point, resembling a knife. Despite Charles's accounting acumen, the man couldn't do a personal errand. He took care of the most complicated tax returns and assisted her with tricky deductions, but Tara suspected she had spent more time buying him organic pastries and getting his dry cleaning than she would have researching the tax code for those questions.

She pushed herself away from her desk and stood in the doorway to Leslie's office. "What can I help you with?"

"I need to access the previous returns for the Barnstein account. I want to see how their depreciation has been handled."

Tara stepped into the office to look at the file open on the desk. "It's not in the printouts?"

"No. Not the breakout. There's a lump sum, and I can't tell how long some of their equipment has been depreciated."

That was strange. Leslie always kept a printed record of purchase dates for equipment, but anyone could make a mistake. "Okay. There should be a depreciation schedule in their client folder."

"I checked. I didn't see one." He took a sip of his coffee with the twelve drops of Bavarian cream in it. "Perhaps it is in Leslie's private files."

"I'll log in to her account, then email you the file. If I find it." She glanced at the clock, stepping toward the door. "I have a client coming in a few minutes."

"Why don't you log me in here and I'll look for it."

Squicky. That was the only way to describe how she felt about Charles nosing around in Leslie's files. But what choice did she have? He needed to finish that return, and she had other work to do. This was the simplest and quickest way. "Okay."

Charles wheeled his chair away from the desk to give Tara room to access the keyboard. She stepped in front of him and performed the necessary operations on the computer. As she waited for the system to restart, Charles eased his chair closer to her. The castors squeaked ominously. Tara made a mental note to have Mark oil them.

"I think you have a lot of potential," Charles said, talking mostly to her posterior.

"Thank you." Tara wasn't sure what he was referring to,

but she'd take a compliment. It was the only nice thing he'd said to her. Leslie gave her great feedback all the time, but it would be nice to hear it from someone she didn't know as well.

"You could do so much better than this place." Charles leaned forward. His gaze inched up her legs. She wanted to swat it away like a biting fly. "In the city, there are so many opportunities, especially for an attractive woman like you."

The computer chirped that the login screen was now available. Tara glanced to the side to check the location of Charles's hands, then typed the necessary information into the computer.

"I happen to like it here." She punched the enter key. "You should be all set. Logout when you're done, and you'll be able to get back to your server space."

"If you change your mind, I'd be happy to exchange favors."

Tara plastered a grimace-like smile on her face and tried to return to her desk. Charles had inched his chair so close to her she couldn't escape without brushing against his knees.

"I better get back to my desk. I have a return to finish before the client arrives."

Charles nodded, but didn't move. What was she supposed to do – climb over his lap? No doubt exactly what he intended.

This had to be the day she'd chosen the narrow, black pencil skirt that didn't allow less than lady-like movements, but she had paired it with her favorite spike-heeled pumps. She lifted her foot, intending to jam it down on his Italian leather encased foot, but she caught her toe on the caster of his chair and lost her balance. She tumbled forward, directly into this chest.

"Well now." Charles chuckled. "Right now? It'll have to be quick, but I'm sure I can manage." He reached for her waist. Before she could extricate herself, the bell on the front door rang. She shoved herself off Charles's chest in time to see Ryan limp in. She gave Charles an extra hard push and stumbled away from him. From the squeal elicited from Charles, her heel had finally found its intended target.

The look on Ryan's face said it all. She had a good idea what the kerfuffle with Charles must have looked like. Why did these things always happen to her? When a nice guy was on the radar she looked a like a floozy. Granted she hadn't much cared a few years before, but she had worked hard to cultivate a professional image and these embarrassing situations still happened all too frequently.

"Sorry if I'm interrupting something," Ryan said. "I'm early."

"Not at all." Tara tried to settle her rattled nerves, but seeing Ryan jumbled them in a totally different way. She smoothed her skirt and ran her hand over her hair. Everything appeared to be in place.

She was going to have to talk to Leslie about Charles. Surely this was a side of him Leslie didn't know about. After Ryan left, she'd give Leslie a call. Then she remembered she'd have to pass the information through Mark. Mark was a good friend, but she didn't feel comfortable talking to him about Charles's innuendos and advances.

Tara knew how to defend herself in these types of situations, but he was Leslie's friend. She'd give him the benefit of the doubt until she heard more about Leslie's condition. She didn't want to offend Leslie by introducing him to her right hook.

"I've got your return all set. Why don't you have a seat and we'll go over it?" Tara gestured to the chair beside her desk. She straightened her jacket, then sat down and woke up her computer. "This will only take a minute. I like to have the computer file up, so we can make any necessary changes or corrections as we talk. It seems to go more smoothly." The hourglass spun on her screen. "So, how's it been going?"

Ryan unzipped his windbreaker and shifted in his seat. "Not bad. I was hoping to run into you at the library again."

Did that mean he wanted to see her again or did he think she was vegging out in front of the television every night? "I know I sound like a broken record, but it's been so busy here. Charles is helping with the complicated returns, but I still do the filing with the IRS. I've been stuck here until after ten most nights."

"I'm sorry this is taking so long. I don't know what's wrong." She tapped her fingers against the mouse pad. Why couldn't his return simply pop up? She wanted him out of here, so she could have a moment to breathe. He had to be contemplating what he might have interrupted. It was so embarrassing. She wanted to shout, "It wasn't anything." But doing so would imply that she was nervous about what she was doing and what he thought about it. She didn't want to give him the satisfaction on either account.

"The IRS servers are probably getting bogged down with so many returns coming in." Ryan picked up a pencil and bounced it on the eraser. The stupid computer was giving her long enough to wonder why she cared. Ryan had been so easy to talk to and so encouraging. She hated feeling like she disappointed him. Even if the incident wasn't her fault, she frustrated herself. Maybe the only way to be taken seriously in accounting would be to have her implants removed, but the thought of another surgery filled her with dread.

"It wasn't what it looked like. I tripped," she said. Her voice felt higher pitched than normal.

"I don't think it's any of my business." He studied his fingernails.

She wanted to shake him. *I thought we had connected at the library. You acted like you saw more to me!*

The hourglass still spun.

"Soo..." What to talk about? Besides her propensity for failure. His T-shirt had a pig with wings on it. "Cool T-shirt.

Where'd you get it?"

He glanced down. "It came with the race entry."

"How far is a marathon anyway?" she asked, reading the lettering on the shirt. "Isn't that like a hundred miles?"

"Twenty-six point two. Slightly shorter than a hundred. I finished third." Ryan put the pencil back on her desk.

"You're kidding."

Ryan shook his head and moved his bad leg. He winced. "I've run twenty-nine and a half marathons."

"Is that when you hurt your leg?"

"No. My first chance at the Boston Marathon was the half. I didn't drink enough fluids and collapsed from dehydration at mile twenty-one. In the middle of Heartbreak Hill."

"I can't imagine running one mile, let alone twenty-one and still having five to go. I think I would cry about any hill."

"That's why they call it Heartbreak Hill. It's a long, hard hill, and lots of runners cry as they climb it. But when you make it, you are so close to the end."

"But you've obviously done other marathons since then. You probably ran the Boston one again and zipped right to the top of the hill."

Ryan wiped his hand over his face. "How long is this going to take?"

Tara checked the computer. "I don't get it. It never takes this long to load. I'll see what Charles is doing. Maybe his files are lagging, too. We might have to reset the server. Sorry. We've never had problems like this."

Tara stood and smoothed her skirt. Okay, Boston and marathons, touchy subjects. Well, she didn't particularly like talking about dance routines and half-time shows anymore either. She walked back to Charles's door. He was hunched in front of the computer with a stack of files beside him. She didn't remember bringing them to him and he usually didn't dig out the prior returns himself. Maybe the spiked heel to the foot had done some good after all. "Are you having computer problems? My computer won't load anything."

Charles shook his head. "Everything's working fine for me." As if whatever was going on was all her fault. She sighed and returned to her desk. Ryan slouched in the seat, his left leg straight out.

"I didn't mean to pry about the marathon."

She could chalk this up to another opportunity blown. No wonder the Ladies couldn't work their magic for her. She had a talent for dousing the relationship before a spark had a chance to flare.

Charles returned the files to the back room.

Ryan shifted in his seat and eased his knee into a different position. "Have you ever had a problem like this before?"

Tara shook her head. "Our system is usually pretty quick. I set up a login for Charles when he arrived. Maybe I did it wrong. I haven't had to do it very often."

"Would you like me to take a look? I have some experience with computer networks and programs."

Maybe she hadn't blown it after all. She couldn't keep the gratitude and relief out of her voice. "That would be awesome. If it stays like this, I'll be behind all day. The server is back this way." Tara stood and headed toward the break room. The server was in a little closet beside the futon. The creak of Ryan's crutches followed her down the hallway. She pulled open the door to the closet and slid out the keyboard tray. "Here it is."

Ryan maneuvered himself in front of the keyboard. He tapped a handful of keys and a login screen appeared. Tara slipped in front of him and typed in the current password. "It changes every two weeks."

"Good thinking. Much more difficult to hack." He navigated to the user administration. "Everything looks fine here. Do you take care of all this?"

"Not really. I know how to do what I know how to do. I try not to mess with anything else. We have a tech guy who installed everything and he's good about answering questions, but we haven't had many problems."

Ryan flashed through a few more screens. "The system is well set up. It's easy to find what I'm looking for."

"What are you looking for?" Tara leaned closer to his shoulder. He smelled like fresh air and green, things she wouldn't be enjoying much of until after the fifteenth.

A list of file names and numbers flashed across the screen. "These are the server logs. They tell what files have been accessed and when. I'm looking for large files that would cause your server to slow down."

Tara recognized the names on the files. "Those are old client returns from last year or before."

"The file sizes are pretty small, so it shouldn't have created a problem."

"Could someone have hacked in? There are bank account and social security numbers in those files." Tara couldn't imagine what a security breach like that would do to them. No one would have their taxes done here again. She clutched the sleeve of Ryan's shirt. The warmth of his body through the cotton comforted her even as her pulse pounded in her ears.

"No. This server isn't connected to the Internet. No one outside the building could get in. It looks like a lot of files were accessed in a short amount of time and the server couldn't handle it."

Tara heaved a sigh of relief. "Charles was looking for some depreciation schedules. He must have had too many files open at once."

"Probably it." Ryan slid a comforting smile her way and clicked a few more things. "It looks like the system maintenance hasn't been running the way it should. I could clean it up for you. It would speed things up."

Tara debated for a moment. Should she let Ryan into the

computer system when she didn't know what he was doing? "Let me check with Leslie. She may have something lined up with the company we purchased this from. If this is straightened out, we can get back to your return," she said, reluctant to leave the relative calm of Ryan's presence.

They hiked back to her desk. "Here we go," Tara said. The return popped up on her screen as quickly as it should have. She reviewed the return with Ryan, fixed some transposed numbers and added the return to the queue to be sent out at the end of the day.

"Your refund should be in your account in two weeks. You said earlier there were deductions you thought your previous accountant had missed. If you bring in those forms and any related receipts, we can see about filing an amended return. Maybe even get you some money back."

"That'd be great." Ryan stood slowly, easing his weight on his bad leg. He took the file Tara handed him.

"I won't be able to get to them before the fifteenth, but they aren't under any deadline anyway. It was good to see you again." Tara stood also.

Ryan nodded and headed for the door. His knee must have stiffened while sitting because his steps hitched more than usual. Shouldn't his walking be improving rather than the other way around?

Chapter Nine

Ryan would be thankful when the weather was finally warm enough to wear shorts, so he didn't have to struggle with his pant leg and his knee brace. He also wouldn't have to strip into these nasty, gap-backed hospital gowns for every appointment.

The paper on the exam table crinkled under his boxers every time he moved, but his leg ached less out of the brace. The padded bands around his calf and thigh left red impressions on what used to be muscle. The skin on his left leg had a soft, fleshy look rather than the rigid, muscular appearance he was familiar with. Even his right leg, despite the extra work it did, had a flabbier texture. They didn't even look like his own legs.

Maybe Dr. Rose would finally okay him for walking without crutches. He'd been on crutches for six long months. He expected to be walking with a cane at least. Most people were rocking the elliptical six months after surgery.

There was a soft knock at the door, then it opened. The doctor stepped through in teal scrubs under a lab coat with a tablet computer tucked under his arm. He sat on a wheeled stool and put the tablet across his knees.

"How's the recovery going?"

"Not as quickly as I'd like." Ryan shifted and the paper crinkled.

"It never does." He scooted forward and studied Ryan's knee. He did a couple of range of motion tests and Ryan winced. The doctor pursed his lips. "Not what I was expecting to see."

"What?" Cold froze his veins and he shivered.

"You shouldn't have that much pain." Dr. Rose grabbed the tablet and pulled up Ryan's chart. He tapped through a couple screens, then scowled. He swiped to another page, then asked, "Did you have an X-ray done today?" When Ryan answered in the affirmative, he stood and kicked the stool back to the counter. "I'll be right back."

Ryan was left in the room with not even the ticking of the clock to mark the passing of time. Every moment felt like twenty. What was the doctor checking? What would he say? Another two weeks on crutches? Three? Was something else wrong?

Ryan's armpits screamed at the thought. He tried to talk himself into liking the idea of more recovery, but he couldn't wrap his head around it. The down time was driving him nuts as it was. He needed running as an outlet for his competitive spirit and the pedestrian exercises from the physical therapist didn't cut it. He twisted the paper under his butt until it no longer crinkled. His fingernail found a crack in the padded vinyl and he picked at it, scratching his nail across the tear. His nail caught, then bumped free. Before that stopped distracting him, the doctor returned with his tablet in front of him like a clipboard.

"I got the new images for your knee sent over." He hooked the stool with his foot and swung it in front of the exam table. "The good news is that your ACL is healing well. It's looks exactly as I would expect."

Ryan had a brief moment of hope amid his irritation at sitting on a glorified toilet seat cover for the better part of the afternoon, but then Dr. Rose had said good news, implying there was bad news to balance it.

"However, we can see the extent of the damage to your cartilage better on these." The doctor shook his head. "Now that the inflammation and swelling has gone down, we get a clearer picture. Your cartilage is almost completely gone."

"Cartilage?" The word rolled in Ryan's stomach like a cheeseburger during a run.

Dr. Rose turned the tablet toward Ryan. "See here. The cartilage is worn almost completely. There's no cushion there."

Ryan squinted at the black and white X-ray on the screen. The doctor drew his fingers apart and the image enlarged. Black filled the space.

"I don't know what I'm looking at," Ryan said. *Nor do I know what it means, other than news I don't want to hear.*

The doctor set the tablet on the counter and picked up a model of a knee joint. "See, this here is your ACL. It stabilizes the knee, especially in side to side motions and direction changes. In most cases, it can be repaired and the patient can return to serious running in about a year."

Ryan nodded. The doctor had explained it all before his surgery. Granted, he'd focused on the time-line for when he would be able to walk without crutches and start running rather than the nitty-gritty of his anatomy. Six months to run, a year to be in top shape. He'd spent half the appointment calculating how he'd map out his training and ignoring the surgeon.

"Inside your knee, cushioning your steps is cartilage." The doctor shifted his stool to come beside Ryan and turned the model. "Now, here is where the cartilage should be. When it's not there, you have bone rubbing on bone. Not very comfortable any time you bend your knee."

That cheeseburger was morphing into a rancid sandwich

on a boat ride. At best, the implications of the doctor's words were not something Ryan wanted to consider. At any other point in the continuum, they were devastating.

"What can happen, especially in long distance runners, is that this cartilage or cushion wears away much faster than it should." The doctor attempted to laugh. "Well, ideally, it should never wear out, but — as in your case — it has worn down to nearly nothing. I imagine your right knee is in similar condition or not far from it."

"So what's this mean? What's the treatment? How long before I can run again?" Only the last question held any importance. He'd do whatever — therapy, surgery, medication — they put him through to be able to run again.

Dr. Rose swiped through a couple screens, skimming the information. "As far as pain management goes, ibuprofen as needed. Physical therapy can help strengthen the muscles around the bone, but you will still have the bone on bone contact with every footfall."

Okay, he got that. It wasn't like he had missed the agony of every step. "But what do I need to do to run?"

He waited to hear about another surgery, another round of physical therapy, another year away from training. None of which he wanted to contemplate, but he would tackle it if it meant another chance at Boston or the Olympic trials.

The doctor tapped the home button on the tablet and the screen went blank. He studied Ryan until Ryan wondered if they were having a staring contest.

"I won't say never because you are young and who knows what medical advances there will be in your life-time, but with the current technology..." He shook his head. "Your best option for even walking without pain is a knee replacement."

"And I would be able to run with a new knee?" Ryan interrupted. If he couldn't do marathons anymore, he'd settle for something shorter. Tune his speed skills and come back as a 10K runner. Or a 5K. He could do the steeplechase. It was only three thousand meters. No, jumping the hurdles wouldn't be good. But a 5K, he could make that enough.

"The replacements only last so many steps, so we don't recommend long distance running. And man, you are only thirty. Under the best circumstances, replacements last about fifteen years. We can do a revision surgery where we replace the replacement. But that surgery is harder to recover from. And, best case scenario, those would wear out when you are sixty. Given how healthy the rest of your body is, you would have a lot of life yet with bad knees."

Ryan lifted the offending leg off the paper, and shifted it to the side. The hamburger that had bounced in his stomach earlier smoldered like charcoal and sank deeper in his gut.

"Running is not an option if you want to walk." The doctor held Ryan's gaze again, seeming to wait for some acknowledgment that Ryan understood.

Never run again.

The words themselves were comprehensible, but he couldn't fathom their meaning all together.

"We'll hold out as long as we can on the surgery. Until then, we'll work on pain management and arresting the deterioration." The doctor kept talking, but Ryan heard little more than droning. He couldn't focus on anything except the no running part.

What would he do without being able to run? Who would he be?

Who would he be?

The question filled his head, leaving no room for answers.

Chapter Ten

After lying in bed tossing and turning for the better part of the night and waking up after short bursts of anxious sleep, he needed to burn off the haze.

The doctor's words rattled around in his head. *You won't run again.* He couldn't cement the prognosis into his reality. He tried to travel forward, beyond the agitation, away from the news, but continually circled back to when his next run would be, how he would ease back into training, what race would be his re-entry into competition.

Then he'd remember.

He wished the doctor was wrong. A second opinion, that's what he needed. Another specialist would see it all more optimistically and recommend a treatment. But why wait for two weeks and another terrifying twenty minutes on a crinkling exam table? He could run now. He'd get all the answers he needed.

A good run would settle his brain. *It always did.*

He looked out the window. The cool, damp morning air called to him. He wanted to be enveloped by the light fog with the pound of his footsteps driving out the anger and frustration.

He donned his favorite T-shirt whose fabric was so worn it was as light as air and laced up his running shoes, reveling in their familiar hug on his feet.

He abandoned his cane by the garage and hop-stepped down the driveway, anxious to be rid of the lethargy in his unexercised body. At the end of the driveway, the pain and frustration faded away. He was a runner. Alone with his miles.

His limp-steps to the sidewalk lengthened into a running stride. He moved tentatively, bracing for the pain. As his left foot rolled through the next step, he placed his right foot more confidently. His body remembered, despite the inactivity and the injury. His body remembered what it was meant to do.

He slid into his normal gait, the easy stretching steps. He felt comfort in the rhythmic movement. There was no pain in his knee.

He felt like himself for the first time in six months.

It barely lasted a block. The agony flared like white lightning, slicing from his knee to his hip. Scorching with each footfall, but he focused down the road, willing the pain back to its depths. His mental strength fought but the weakness and pain chomped at his leg with razor-sharp teeth. After ten more steps, his knee crumpled, and he skidded into the sidewalk. His body scraped across the cement which skinned his shins, knees, and palms.

He braced his hands on the ground, closed his eyes, and inched his right foot under his weight. Pushing to a stand, he balanced on his good leg. He eased weight over to his left leg. Touching his toe to the ground, his eyes started watering. He gritted his teeth and settled his weight.

You won't run again. The words hurt more than his knee, but he could ignore words. Another deep breath, then he pushed off to run again. His leg collapsed as soon as his weight was on it. He tumbled forward. His chin ground into the cement, jarring his teeth as he came to rest against a crack in the sidewalk. He hit hard enough to rattle his brain and knock some sense into it. This was it. *Rock bottom.* The doctor was right. If he tried to run, he wouldn't be able to walk.

He lay there, letting the air filter back into his lungs and the burn flare on his face. It was early enough that no one else was up to observe his failure.

He dragged himself to a sitting position and examined the damage. Blood dribbled down his shins and gravel clung to his palms. He brushed the back of his hand across his chin and earned a smear of red across his skin.

He'd tripped while running before and suffered equally ugly cases of road rash. The humiliation that came with this particular case was a first. Other times, he'd caught himself, rolled, and was back on his feet without losing more than a second or two from his pace. This time he couldn't get back on his feet. Wasn't sure how he would get back home. Wasn't sure about anything.

He shuffle-scooted to the greening grass, wincing each time he flexed his knee, then collapsed on the neighbor's yard. He couldn't even run a block. He'd never run a marathon or a 5K or even a mile again. He rubbed his bloodied hand against his eyes.

Running was the one thing that made him feel alive, like he was someone special. Now he didn't even have that.

He had no job, no home, no friends.

The only fresh start he'd thought he had was with Tara.

Tara. He groaned. He'd meant her to be a distraction until he got through all this crap and now this crap was never going to end. If his need for distraction wasn't going to end, what about his need for her? Another question he couldn't answer.

He pounded his fist into the ground and struggled to get back on his feet without bending his knee or putting any weight on the bad leg. It was impossible.

He finally managed to crawl close enough to a mailbox and used the post to pull himself to his feet. Even then, the feat took some awkward contortions and was probably a hilarious show for any neighbor spying on him over her perking coffee. He hopped-stepped toward home on his right foot, stopping to catch his breath every ten steps. Would he ever get back on both his feet?

His mom scrambled down the driveway, waving his cane as he cleaved to his own mailbox.

"The neighbor called and said you fell." Her bathrobe flapped behind her and her slippers flopped on the pavement. There was a day when the sight of his mother in her bathrobe outside the house would have had him around the block in embarrassment, but this morning it was exactly what he needed. "Oh sweetheart," she gasped when she was close enough to see the road rash. "Are you all right?"

Ryan shrugged and grabbed his cane. She slipped under his shoulder and supported him to the house.

Chapter Eleven

Ryan dug through the boxes of paperwork he had shoved into his mother's basement. His tax returns had to be in here somewhere. The search was supposed to distract him from the infinite cycle of asking himself what he was going to do now. No answer filled in after the blinking cursor of his brain. He had found endorsement contracts, newspaper clippings, and dog-eared pages of programming code, but not any IRS 1040s or their associated paperwork.

Tara had said she wouldn't be able to look over his stuff until after the fifteenth, but dropping off his forms would give him a chance to see her again and get his mind off his prognosis. He pictured her coming out of Charles's office after the slimeball had tripped her. Her cheeks had been flushed with embarrassment, but she'd managed to hold onto her cool and get on with her job. That was mental toughness whether she saw it in herself or not.

Mental tenacity was something he seemed to be severely lacking in today. One minute he wallowed in the loss of his gift, the next he pondered moving on. If he could block the news out and forget he had been so close to realizing his dreams about winning the Boston Marathon and going to the Olympics, maybe he could survive. He'd stay in that belief for a few minutes, but the strength to maintain it always failed. He wondered if the doctor was wrong, if there was a surgery that could fix him, or if he'd wake up in a cold sweat having dreamed the horror of the last six months.

He flipped the lid off the next box and dropped the cover to the floor. It bumped his cane from its resting spot against the tower of boxes. He glanced at it then focused on the box. This one was more organized. Manila envelopes lined the interior, but a heavy, linen one had been abandoned on top. He stared at it, knowing exactly what it contained.

They'd sent it as soon as his ACL tear was confirmed. They couldn't carry an athlete who would be out of competition for a year.

It was the letter terminating his contract with the track club. His fingers still trembled when he reached for it. The biggest dream and goal he'd had for the last decade and one letter ended it. It looked so innocuous in its creamy linen paper and nondescript font. Receiving it had hurt worse than the injury to his knee. He stabbed the letter into the side of the box.

"Ryan!" his mother called as she clomped down the steps. "Since you're down here, could you do me a favor?"

"Sure. What do you need?" Ryan ran his fingers over the edges of the folders until he recognized the one holding his tax returns. He yanked it out of the box and dropped it to the floor. It hit the faded linoleum and spun away.

"I'd like to clear out some stuff down here, so there's some open space." His mother stood in front of the old console television where he'd played video games. When she'd moved to Carterville from Glendale, all the stuff she hadn't wanted to part with ended up in the basement. "I want to make some room for an exercise bike."

Ryan was thankful he'd been leaning against the pile of

boxes or he would have landed on his can. His mother and an exercise bike? Something weird was going on here. She'd even given up her nightly bowl of ice cream and replaced it with a dainty scoop of frozen yogurt. Whatever the reason for this fitness kick, she was definitely looking better. She'd lost a few pounds and she seemed to have more energy.

"It's being delivered tomorrow, and I want to put my yoga mat over here too."

An exercise bike *and* a yoga mat? Perhaps his mother was preparing for the zombie apocalypse. He laughed to himself. It was as reasonable as any other explanation she could come up with.

Ryan surveyed the basement. The boxes he'd brought from his apartment and his stuff from high school barely took up a few feet of the cramped floor space. The rest was random furniture that didn't fit with the decor upstairs and the remnants of his mother's various jump-started hobbies. When she discovered something new, she went in head-first and got every tool or whatever related to it. As she lost steam, the accoutrements ended up in the basement, waiting for someone to revive them.

"As long as I don't have to go up and down the stairs." The thought of descending the seventeen steps to the basement made him wince. Funny how going down stairs was actually worse than going up.

"We can stack it up by the slider. Then I can drive my car around back and load it up."

"Why don't we load it in the back of my SUV? You won't be able to fit these boxes in your little car."

Neither of them was in good enough shape to carry any of the furniture, but they wedged and kicked the console TV across the room, scarring the linoleum.

"Oh well, here you are. This must be all your school stuff." His mother led him around the stacks of boxes and paraphernalia they had collected over the years to a pile of boxes labeled 'Ryan.' "Put what you don't want in the pile over there. I don't know how we collected so much stuff."

Ryan tugged apart the interlocked top of the cardboard box. A wave of dust floated into his face. He coughed. How long had his mom been keeping this around? He bent the top pieces down along the sides. His kindergarten finger-paintings covered the top of the box. No need for these. He doubted anyone at the thrift store would want them either.

He reached farther into the box and discovered a ring of finisher ribbons. He fingered the faded silk from the Old Fashioned Days Midget Mile, chuckling to himself. They should have called it a dash. A rambunctious crowd of eight, nine, and ten-year-olds with no notion of how far a mile was. They leapt from the starting line expecting to run as fast as they could the whole way. They were gasping and stumbling less than halfway through the course. He among them — but the running bug had bitten him. A mile had been an unfathomable distance to travel on foot back then. Who could run so far?

He set the ribbons aside and next found his varsity letter from high school. He'd lettered in both cross country and track, but he'd never purchased the leather jacket. It seemed like a football or baseball player thing because they had the muscles to fill out the rigid fabric. He'd tried one on, but the heavy leather felt wrong on his frame — like wearing the lead shield for an X-ray. He hadn't considered himself an athlete back then. Running was something he had to do. It wasn't a sport as others might describe. Then he was running miles each day, some easy, some full out.

Miles had become a measure of the day's run rather than a single goal. When had he lost the appreciation for something so simple – the basic integer of his passion?

Now he longed to run a mile, a lap around the track, even a hundred meter dash. And barring a medical miracle, he'd never do it again.

He placed the letter aside. That was something he'd keep. He dug further in the box. An old pair of running spikes, a baseball cap, and a stack of newspapers. He'd run his first 5K in those spikes. The leather on the shoes crumbled in his hands. Not worth preserving. He dropped them in the garbage pile. The baseball cap went into the sale pile. The newspapers. He didn't remember saving them. He paged through the first one and found nothing worth saving. There was a coupon for the local shoe store, but it was fifteen years old. He chucked the papers and moved on to the next box.

T-shirts. Every silk-screened shirt for every race he'd entered. The shirts had attracted the musty smell of the basement and the delicate texture of worn-to-death fabric. They were almost transparent and yellowed from age and sweat. The first ones he'd won he wore until the back and shoulders had giant holes. Later, he'd done so many races, he barely wore the shirts more than a couple times before he outgrew them. He unfolded one. When had he ever been this small? He checked the date on the shirt. He'd been in high school, so not middle school as he'd hoped. No wonder everyone picked on him. He looked like a fifth grader until his senior year when he'd hit a growth spurt and grew almost five inches in one year. The added height wasn't much better. Long, wiry limbs, dangling from a ribcage. Not an ounce of fat softened his frame and his face was all sharp angles. No one Tara would give a second glance.

The other Tara he'd met at that bonfire hadn't. He scratched his nose and set the shirt down. She'd shoved him aside and dashed off with the head of the football team. Story of his high school career.

Luckily he'd started to fill out in college when he added weight lifting to his training. A light breeze wouldn't knock him over anymore. He had a thicker body to match his sinewy legs and arms.

He put the shirt back in the box. These couldn't go to a

thrift store. They were little more than rags to anyone who didn't care.

"What's all that?" His mom eyed the growing pile of cotton rags at his feet. She came closer. "All your running stuff. You've had quite a career, Ryan."

"It feels like I was just getting started." He slid the last T-shirt to the side and saw the wrinkled ribbons and tarnished silver of the trophies and medals he had won over the years.

"It stinks it had to end this way, but you did things so many people only dream about." She took the top shirt off the pile on the floor and smoothed the crumpled printing. "Now you can start a new dream."

He'd known it would come someday. Like when he was forty and he stopped competing for the top places in the race and focused on the medals in his age group. He'd run then for the joy of being with other runners. Enjoying the sun on his skin, or the splatter of rain against his face and the splash of a puddle as he stomped through. He'd braved all types of weather, in every time of year. In Michigan it was possible to run in shorts on Christmas and gloves and pants on the Fourth of July.

He wadded up the rest of the shirts and shoved them into a box, then slid the box of medals off the stack. He jabbed it over to the slider, alternating with his good leg and his cane. "I don't know who I am without running."

"You are the same person you've always been." She patted him on the shoulder, then gave him a gentle squeeze. "Big changes aren't ever easy. When I moved here from Glendale after your father died, I didn't think life would ever be as good. I still miss him every day, but I've found new adventures to fill it. You need to find a different pursuit to be passionate about."

Tara's laugh flashed through his mind. While he was passionate about her, loving her wouldn't pay the bills. He needed a career, something to show her he wasn't a crippled failure.

The next box was filled with Matchbox cars and the burned-out leftovers of a model rocket. That could go. He shoved the box to the side. The last box was crammed full of DOS code manuals, and green and white printouts of software programs he'd dabbled with in high school. In college, he'd tackled HTML and Java, then played with Flash during his downtime over the last few years. These manuals weren't worth the paper they were printed on anymore. Did new computer programmers even know what DOS was?

His mom had only one more box to go to the thrift store. It didn't help her clear out the space for the aerobics troupe or whatever crazy plan she was attempting.

He maneuvered the box of cars onto the handcart his mother had discovered in the piles of junk over to the sliding door. He wandered over to the pile of records his mom had been sorting.

"I wish my phonograph still worked. There's some good stuff here. What are all these papers?" She kicked the stack of manila envelopes by Ryan's feet.

"Old tax returns. Tara wanted to go over them. She said I might be able to deduct some more things."

"Tara's such a hard worker. How's she holding up without Leslie in the office?"

"She'd probably be doing fine if Charles wasn't there."

His mother gave him a contemplative look, then opened another box. She pushed some balled up newspaper to the side. "Who is Charles?"

Ryan bent over a box of vintage vinyl and skeptically studied the bands he didn't recognize. He straightened and rolled his shoulders back. His muscles and bones snapped and popped into new positions. "Some guy who is supposed to be doing the complicated returns, but I think he's a waste of time. He's got Tara running all over town on errands when he's not trying to look down her blouse."

The urge to break something surprised him. Ryan imagined Charles did that to a lot of people. But Ryan's reaction was different. He wanted to protect Tara because she was the only one who understood what he was going through. The frustration he felt at not being able to do something he loved.

The question bubbled to the surface again. Tara? His brain continued to waffle. She was hot. He was a mess. She was amazing. Beautiful, confident, encouraging, intelligent. Every time he saw her, something about her blew him away. What would she see in him? She'd been a cheerleader with her pick of the football team. He was nothing but a scrawny has-been who could barely walk. He couldn't keep himself in one frame of mind for more than a few minutes. Was it fair or even right to involve someone else in his carnival of emotions?

"Mom." He was probably going to shoot himself for asking her for help, but his mother knew Tara. He could use all the advice he could get. Crazy or not.

"When did you start your aerobics classes?" He rolled the box on its corners to the hand truck and wheeled it over to the slider. That wasn't the question he planned to ask, but maybe the conversation would swing in his direction and he wouldn't have to bring it up directly.

"We've been meeting for a couple months now, but The Ladies want to go back to our normal Friday meetings after the library charity auction."

"Are they going to stop exercising?"

"No, just change the location."

"What's wrong with the library meeting room? It has a great open space."

"Son, it has windows." She lifted another album and tilted it toward the light, then stuffed it back in the box. "Some of us have parts that shake too much for spectators."

Ryan dismissed that image before it had a chance to etch into his brain.

"What spurred the exercise kick?" He flipped through the albums in the box his mom had abandoned. Nothing piqued his interest.

His mother didn't answer right away.

"Have you been to see a doctor lately? Is there something you aren't telling me?" he asked. Could her sudden venture into athletic fitness be caused by an underlying health problem?

"Oh no, sweetie, nothing like that. I'm as right as rain. It's an idea we had to help the library."

"Help the library? How does aerobics help the library?" Was his mother in the early stages of dementia? He wasn't following this train of thought at all. It was even more bizarre than the ideas usually generated by her friends.

His mother waved her hand, dismissing his question. "I meant we got the idea at the library while we were talking about fundraising."

Ryan still didn't get the connection between the library, fundraising, and his mother's new-found interest in aerobics and cycling. But she was nodding so emphatically, he felt himself nodding too. Maybe it was better to pretend he had a clue what she was talking about rather than risk more confusion.

He hand-trucked a couple more boxes over to the slider, then slumped on the threadbare sofa. He had been standing for too long. His leg would scream at him for the rest of the day.

His mother ambled over and plopped down next to him. "I thought this exercise stuff was supposed to give you more energy, but I'm beat. How do you do it?"

"It takes a while to build up endurance."

"More than a couple weeks, eh?" His mom elbowed his shoulder.

"Yep. But it's a whole lot easier to lose what you've gained." His thoughts drifted to the shrinking muscles in his left leg. It didn't take long at all.

"Well, I need a boost. Would you like some coffee?"

"Don't make it just for me." Ryan already had his usual cup today, but he no longer had to worry about what the extra caffeine would do to his training.

"Oh I always have a cup this time of the afternoon. Cookies, too." She moved another box of discarded albums to the floor beside the back doorway and headed up the stairs to the kitchen. "Probably should skip those though."

Ryan grabbed his cane and pushed himself to his feet, mentally preparing himself to tackle the stairs. "So your friends have branched out from matchmaking then?" he called as he gritted his teeth through each step. There, good question. It should lead him around to discussing what he should do about Tara.

"Not entirely." She filled the carafe with water, then poured it into the coffeemaker.

"Can I ask if I've been discussed at any of these meetings?" Maybe they already had some ideas for him. One way or the other.

"You can ask." His mom measured the coffee grounds and poured them into the coffee maker.

"But I'm not going to get an answer." He settled at the kitchen table, his knee screaming after the jaunt up the stairs.

"Nope. All meetings are confidential." She said it like they were debating the formula for cold fusion.

After pouring two cups of coffee and placing them on the table, she filled a plate of cookies and placed it in front of Ryan. "I shouldn't eat any of those, but they're here." Scraping a chair across the kitchen floor, she selected a chocolate chip cookie. "It's so nice to have you home. Even if it is because you broke your leg."

He spun his coffee cup. He'd been stalling long enough with his questions about his mom and her group. He needed to ask about Tara.

"What else is going on in town?" He chickened out. Again. Some things he couldn't discuss with his mother.

Chapter Twelve

Tara shivered in front of the dairy display, studying the various containers for an organic, hormone-free cream cheese. Simply grabbing the cheapest wouldn't work as Charles's delicate taste buds would be traumatized, and she'd lose the rest of the afternoon. He wouldn't get anything accomplished while sulking, and she'd have to run over to the health foods store in Glendale to appease him.

She picked up another container and studied the label. It didn't mention whether the dairy products used were from cloned cows or not. A familiar swish whispered up the aisle. Ryan's wind-pants. She instantly swung toward the sound, eager to see Ryan and hear how his appointment went. She hadn't dared to call him the previous evening, though she'd contemplated it several times. Would that be presuming too much about their friendship? She had only known him a little more than a week and didn't want to confuse the excitement of attraction with the first steps of falling in love.

Love.

As that four-letter word crossed her mind, she dropped the cream cheese back in the display as though its nonpasteurized microbes were creeping out. Falling in love? She shouldn't be thinking about Ryan and love. If he got good news from the doctor, he would be returning to training camp soon. While she was happy for his healing, she was reluctant to see him go.

As he came around the castle of bananas, she saw that instead of hunching over his crutches, he was walking gingerly with a cane. The side of his chin sported an angry red scrape.

"Ryan!" she bubbled, feeling a little too much like a giggly, high school girl with a bouncy ponytail. He came to stand beside her. She tentatively touched the scruff near the scratch. "What happened here?"

The jaw under her fingertips tensed. "Slipped on the sidewalk yesterday."

Tara dropped her hand away. Switching from crutches to a cane must be a difficult adjustment.

"I thought Charles would have you tied to your desk by now." His teasing tone was marred by a wince each time he put his weight on his left leg.

"Not when he has a craving for fresh, gluten-free organic bagels with lactose-free cream cheese." She shrugged and snatched up the cheese spread container she had been studying. "You know Charles. Only the most specific and annoyingly hard to find."

Ryan took the container from her. His fingers grazed hers and a delightful zing slipped up her arm. It was enough to make her happy to be at the grocery store on Charles's stupid errand.

"What are his requirements this time? Only Japanese cows?"

"Oh, don't give him any ideas. Organic and hormone-free cows. I thought this errand would be easier."

Ryan chucked the cheese back into the display and selected another container. "This one should do. Does he make you pay for everything, too?"

"Strangely, he doesn't. He gave me a twenty." She pulled it out of her pocket and waved it. "He did demand change and the receipt." She spun the container and gaped at the price sticker. "Good thing too, because I wouldn't shell out six dollars for a fancy cream cheese spread."

She beamed at Ryan. It was so good to see his improvement. A cane today, and he'd probably be running in a week. When he wasn't bent over crutches, his T-shirt stretched across his tall frame and the short sleeves wrapped snuggly around his biceps. He was taller than she expected, too. She had to tilt her face up and her eyes met the scruff on his chin. She imagined she would fit perfectly under his arm. She had to wrap a vise-grip around her brain to keep it from running away with that idea as delightful as it was.

"You must have had good news from the doctor." She tapped the cane he gripped. "This is a step up."

Ryan flexed his hand around the handle and cleared his throat. "Yeah. Monday, actually."

"Oh." She wavered between wanting to know what he found out and being hurt he hadn't called her right away. Good news meant he was leaving, and he must not have gotten as attached as she was. He'd said his stay was temporary, so she had tried not to invest much of her heart in him, but given the sting of this small rejection, she had failed.

From the look on his face, she could tell whatever the doctor said hadn't been what he wanted to hear. Still an upgrade in equipment had to be a little good news.

Ryan's chest heaved as he took a breath and slowly deflated. "Not what I was hoping for."

"No running yet?" She reached out to touch his arm. His muscles tensed into ripped cords. Who knew runners had such strong arms?

"Possibly not ever." The words were tight as if saying them required sawing them from a piece of overcooked steak.

"My ACL seems fine, but the cartilage is gone. I'll be lucky if I can walk without pain."

"They can't do anything?"

"A knee replacement eventually, but he wants me to wait as long as possible."

Tara inched closer, wanting to hug him, but not daring in the middle of the grocery store. His balance with the cane might not be the steadiest, and with her track record, she could send him sprawling into the bananas. "I'm so sorry. I know how much you were hoping for better news."

"Better news?" Ryan snorted. "I would have rather heard my ACL was still mucked up. I can run with a bad ACL."

"The doctor said that?"

Ryan wavered a moment. "Not competing on a world class level, but I'd still be able to run. Now, I can't do anything. Even walking without this—" He waved his cane and sneered. "Walking without this might not be possible."

"You could get one with flames on it," Tara teased, trying to bump him out of his funk. It wouldn't do any good to dwell on the past and what might have been. She'd tried when she'd been cut from the dance team. Each day hoping the management would change its mind about the uniforms or her scars and call her back. She had jumped for the phone each time it jingled. It had taken her months to find her footing. Not until Leslie had hired her had she found a direction or a new purpose.

She had to be Ryan's Leslie.

Ryan shrugged. "I don't know what to think yet. I don't know what I'll do."

Who cared what the town gossips might say? He needed her support right now. She slipped her arm around his waist, squeezing him to her side. He wrapped his arm around her shoulder, holding her tightly to him. She fit snugly there and some of the stress of dealing with Charles eased. "It doesn't feel like it right now, but you'll make it. You have options."

Ryan shook his head. "I can't give up a lifelong dream in the blink of an eye."

"No one's saying you have to, but you are more than a marathoner. You are more than how fast your legs can carry you. Don't you have other dreams?"

He stared away from her as if the tubs of cottage cheese might start a song and dance routine about the importance of calcium for bone development and he didn't want to miss a second of it. Was he hearing anything she said?

"Could you do something running related? Like coaching, developing training plans, or something. You could probably write a mobile phone app to create custom training plans and make millions."

He gave her a skeptical look. "Nothing I've planned for. Nothing that will get me through tomorrow."

"You know all that computer stuff. My only skill was talking on the phone when I lost the cheerleading gig. I floundered for a long time. You'll hit the ground running."

He grimaced.

Not her best tact, but at least he was listening. It was a start. He'd need time for the seed to germinate.

"Sorry, bad choice of words. Just because your life isn't turning out how you planned doesn't mean where it's going is wrong." She studied him, searching for a glimmer of understanding, of hope, or a hint he wouldn't collapse on himself.

She was jealous of all the opportunities he had. But he needed time, she reminded herself.

"I'm sure that will be comforting at some point, but today it's meaningless."

"Yeah." She hugged him tighter, then reluctantly let go. Gave him some space. No matter how good his body felt next to hers. Maybe a change of topic would help, like when she would see him again. A topic of much more interest. "When are you bringing your other papers in?"

"I found the old returns in the basement, but I need to find some other documents. They're down there somewhere, but I'm avoiding stairs as much as possible." His voice was terse.

The basement wasn't the only thing he was avoiding. But she was going to see him again soon. She wasn't going to allow him to wallow in his despair for long.

"Gotcha. Well, bring them in as soon as you get a chance." She waved the cream cheese which had been out of the refrigerated display for longer than something with no preservatives should be. "I better get this to Charles before he or it expires."

Chapter Thirteen

Charles had settled on the futon with his feet on Leslie's body pillow for an afternoon nap. He'd been doing it every day after the lunch rush. Despite all his disparaging of the futon, he made generous use of it. Not in the way he insinuated to Tara, but he'd logged more snoozes there than Leslie had.

Tara closed the door to the break room to block Charles's snoring and scurried back to her desk. She had twenty minutes to tackle the pile on her desk before he woke up and started demanding she run errands for his latest minuscule cravings. Weird cream cheese, chocolate-covered raisins, and super-mint breath fresheners. Each time he only wanted one thing, and he always rolled a shiny new twenty off that stack of his. At least he wasn't trying to expense all his junk. He'd probably send her on another errand as soon as he woke up, but right now she had a stack of 1040s to enter into the computer system.

She opened the first file and tapped away at the keypad. Before she made it halfway through their income statements, the door jangled and Minnie blew in. The gust of wind thumped the door shut behind her. Tara winced, hoping the cacophony of the bells didn't wake Charles from his beauty sleep.

Minnie smoothed her hair and plopped into the seat next to Tara's desk. "How's it going?"

Tara flipped the folder closed and punched the save keys on the computer, knowing her twenty minutes of free time were gone. "Not too bad. We're staying on top of things." It wasn't completely false as long as she referred to herself in the royal 'we.'

"I was up to visit Leslie. She's doing well. May even be able to go home this afternoon." Minnie pulled a compact out of her purse and checked her hair. "This wind did a number on my hairdo. I don't know how they'll ever get it straightened out for the pictures."

"Great news about Leslie. I suppose she will still be on bed rest for the duration."

"That'd be my guess too. Speaking of pictures — do you know where I can find a dunk tank?"

Tara had no idea how Minnie connected pictures to a dunk tank, and probably didn't want to know. "Doesn't the high school have one?"

"Thank you. I didn't even think of that. I need to arrange one for the library benefit."

"I thought it was a black tie event."

Minnie looked at her like she'd questioned the wisdom of putting peanut butter with jelly on a sandwich. *Alrighty then.* It'd go well with the mechanical bull Bubba's Demolition was sponsoring. Leslie had sponsored the drinks, figuring it was an easy way to get people to add a zero or two to their checks.

"The dry cleaner wants to do a 'Dunk a Hunk.' They want the men in tuxes. Maybe they're hoping for a twofer and getting their suits in to be cleaned, too." She screwed up her mouth as if contemplating the business sense. "I promised I'd help rope in some hunks. What's this Charles look like?"

Tara wrinkled her nose.

"Oh well. Yvonne thought Ryan would do it."

The picture of Ryan all wet that jumped into Tara's mind was definitely not safe for work. Although the thoughts incited by the image of Ryan in a tuxedo probably weren't either. Too bad whipping a baseball at him and knocking the 'woe is me' out of his head had almost as much appeal. She wasn't going to let him feel sorry for himself and her fastball hurtling toward his head just might jog him out of his funk.

"Well, I better be off. We're all due at the photographer at one. Have a good afternoon." Minnie disappeared out the door as quickly as the wind blew her in.

Tara grabbed her files, refusing to contemplate the mystery that was Minnie when she had work to do.

Chapter Fourteen

After digging through the basement and talking with his mom, Ryan's brain was fried. As much as he wanted to find a solution to all the things bugging him, his mind was too overloaded to concentrate. Normally, he'd go for a run. The steady rhythm of his feet pounding the pavement shook the jumble into some kind of order. At the end he had a game plan. This morning had proved that was no longer an option. He needed a distraction, so his brain could slow down for a while. Maybe he'd rent a movie.

He drove to the last video store in town. None of his mom's movies appealed to him. Every DVD case featured flowers or some sappy couple embracing in the rain. Not a car chase, explosion, or gunfight among them.

As he drove by Knotts Accounting, he happened to notice the place was still lit up. *You didn't "happen" to notice,* he amended. *You looked, wanting a glimpse of Tara.* He wanted to see her at her desk like a beacon, calling him out of his storm. She could settle his agitated thoughts. She could bring him calm, and remind him how to move through adversity.

She was still in front of her computer. Nine o'clock at

night, and she was still at work? Tax season sucked, but he admired her dedication. Who else would work so hard and put up with so much for a friend?

Ryan stopped at the video store and wandered through the displays. The decent-looking new releases were gone. There were about ten copies of some teeny-bopper thing. He didn't need any reminders of his high school experience. He wove around the older shelves. Most of the movies had been replaced by video games, so even the selection there was sparse. Nothing appealed to him any more than his mother's collection of outdated exercise videos.

He debated whether to pick something randomly and hope for the best or find something else to do. Then he remembered Tara sitting at her desk. If she had been there all day, she could probably use a break. Charles had surely hightailed it hours before. Maybe he could take her something to eat.

It would be a chance to focus on something besides his own misery. And if it didn't, well, the eye candy would be better than the flamboyant exercise videos.

He stopped at Bart's and picked a wide selection from their take out menu, being sure to add a couple of milkshakes, because who didn't like those? Tara's tastes couldn't be judged from their only dinner at Bart's. She'd ordered fries and a hamburger, but hadn't taken a bite after the call from Mark. He took the bags and headed back to her office. The sign said office hours were extended during tax season, but closing time was two hours before. The door was still open, so he let himself in.

"I'll be with you in a moment," Tara said, barely sparing him a glance. She'd wound her hair on top of her head and stuck a couple pencils through it to hold it in place.

"You should lock up. Anyone could waltz in here." He shook the fast food bags; the paper crinkled enticingly.

"Do you have food?" She let go of her mouse and leaned

back in her seat. "I can't lock up until we close. I've got another hour."

"Not according to your sign." He laughed as she scrambled for the clock on her desk.

She pulled it out from under a pile of receipts and rubbed her eyes. "I can't believe it's so late already. Where does the day go?"

"Time flies when you're having fun?" Ryan dropped the bags on the chair beside her desk.

"I wish. This return is giving me fits. Charles filed it this morning, and it keeps bouncing back." Tara shoved the mouse across its pad.

"What's the problem?" Ryan slipped around the desk and skimmed Tara's computer screen. He spared a glance at the blonde curl that looped around her ear and spiraled toward the neckline of her blouse and his thoughts followed it. Any memory of what was on her screen fizzled.

"I don't know. I've double checked all the numbers. The social security numbers match, addresses, everything." She pressed her fingertips to her temples. "Although, I've been looking at it for so long there could be a big red arrow pointing to the problem and I wouldn't see it."

"Then it's a good thing I came. You need a break. I wanted to see if it worked for me to look at the servers tomorrow." It just popped into his head. It was as good an excuse as any should the dinner idea not go over. At least he'd seem less like a stalker. "Bart's. In case you haven't eaten."

Tara's stomach growled in response. She tossed a pencil down on the pile of papers. "How'd you know I was here?"

"I saw the light as I was going to the video store." Ryan shoved his hands in his pockets.

"I haven't rented a move in so long. What'd you get?" Tara rubbed her hand over her forehead.

"Nothing. If I wanted something crappy, I'd have chosen one of my mom's exercise videos."

"I hear ya. Not that I've had time, but I haven't seen a good movie in forever. Why don't we take these to the break room?" She threw herself onto her feet and snatched the bags from the chair. "I don't want to spill anything on my desk."

Ryan followed her down the hall, appreciating the way her skirt slipped across her behind. She deposited the bags on the table and pulled a container of french fries out of one. She kicked off her shoes and prepared to sit on the futon, but she hopped up a moment later.

"I should lock the front door. I don't want anyone else stumbling in." She hurried down the hall in her stocking feet. He swallowed. Suddenly, the office seemed a whole lot more intimate. Her pumps lay on their sides under the table. The high heels made his ankles and other parts ache, but they did wonderful things for her calves.

Tara returned and curled up in the corner of the futon. "I turned down the lights too. Wouldn't want any more wayward clients banging on the doors." She extracted a few more fries. "Thanks for this. I've been missing too many meals lately."

Barefoot, low light, all they needed was some Barry White and the mood would be complete. Just the distraction he needed. "People desperate to have their taxes this late at night?"

"In April, yes. As the fifteenth gets closer, people start panicking."

"I bet that's fun." Nothing related to taxes sounded fun to Ryan, unless it had to do with Tara. Anything with Tara sounded interesting. His mouth watered and it had nothing to do with the smell of hamburgers.

"You're telling me. Leslie and I have talked about installing a video camera for the last week. People waving their hands in front of the door. It's hilarious." She laughed to herself. "It could be we are so tired by then, we're slap happy."

"Do you normally work so many hours during tax season?" Ryan asked, plopping down on the futon, leaving space between himself and Tara to spread out the food. She needed sustenance before he attempted any other stress relief.

"This year I'm obviously working a lot more, but it's always crazy busy. In January we start with forty-five to fifty hour weeks and it escalates from there. There's usually a week or two in March when it slows down in comparison, but it jumps right back up. I don't know how Leslie kept up this year," Tara said between bites of fries. "The baby was supposed to come a little before Leslie takes her long summer vacation."

"At least you have Charles to help out."

Tara rolled her eyes. "I almost think I'd be better off without him. He's got me doing so much other stuff, it's taking me twice as long to do my own work."

Ryan reached for a cheeseburger.

"Is there only one of those?" Tara asked, waving her bitten-in-half fries.

"There's a regular hamburger and a salad." He held the wrapped sandwich toward her. "You want this one?"

Tara nodded. Ryan passed her the sandwich, fished out the extra ketchup and mustard packets, then took the salad for himself.

"I'm so tempted to put a laxative in Charles's coffee, so he'll be in the bathroom for a while and I can get something done without him calling me every two minutes." She crumpled the wrapper and tossed it toward the garbage can. It bumped the rim and tumbled in.

"He might still call for you."

Tara grimaced. "Good point." After another bite of her sandwich, she said, "I don't get why Leslie would recommend him. I've met several of her other accounting associates, and they seem like nice, professional people. People who would get their own coffee, especially if they wanted it with twelve drops of Bavarian cream."

"Have you had a chance to ask Leslie about him?" Ryan polished off the salad and snapped the dressing packet and spork inside the plastic container. He tossed it onto the table, not willing to be shown up by Tara's previous three-pointer.

"No. I haven't even had a chance to call her. Mark's been leaving updates on my voice mail. I hate to bother her when she's supposed to resting. Her blood pressure is already too high."

"You should talk to her. Be casual about it. Something like 'boy, Charles is sure particular about his coffee' and see what she says. You could find out if he's always like this or just with you." Ryan collected the remains of their meal and dumped it in the trash. He settled back on the futon. This time closer to Tara. He slung his arm behind her shoulder, no longer able to resist the curl trailing along her neck.

"That's a good idea. It shouldn't stress her out." Tara reclined on the futon and propped her feet on a chair.

"And if she says he's kind of needy, you'll know he isn't picking on you." He twirled his finger in her hair, grazing the silky smoothness of her skin. She leaned into his touch.

"And if he is?"

"Give it back. He's not helping you out if he's creating more work." He trailed his fingers down her neck. Her skin was as silky as he imagined.

"What if he leaves? We need to have someone who can handle the complicated tax returns. After the tax season, Leslie had someone else arranged as backup."

"So Charles is supposed to leave in a little over a week anyway? You only have to make his life miserable for a few days. It could be your subtle revenge."

"Now there's an option. You've turned me off the laxative thing though." She sipped her chocolate shake, then chewed thoughtfully on the straw.

"Probably for the best. There are other options. Pepper in

his coffee grounds. Junky ink pens in his desk drawer. Pencils with lead that always breaks. A tangled phone cord. A mouse cord just a little too short. A flat spot on the wheel of his chair."

"Those are good. Have you been thinking about this for a while?"

"They're things that would annoy me if I worked here."

"I do have a bunch of barely working pens. I've been meaning to throw them out."

"So where's he staying? There aren't many hotels in Carterville." Ryan shifted his knee and found himself pressed closer to Tara, a situation he didn't mind at all.

"There aren't any. The closest one is in Glendale. There are a few bed and breakfasts."

"My mom's friend, Minnie, owns one, doesn't she?"

"Yeah. The Lilac Bower, but if he was staying there I would have heard. Minnie wouldn't put up with his picky behavior, even if she does try to cater to her guests."

"Is he commuting?"

"Maybe that's his problem. He's tired from driving so much."

"You could suggest a place in town. So he could get more sleep and be less crabby. Although you should probably phrase it a bit more diplomatically."

"'You're a crab, get some sleep!' doesn't work for you?" She swatted his leg playfully.

"Only from my mother." He grabbed her hand and clasped it in his, absently smoothing his thumb over her knuckles.

"Did she get her basement cleaned out? I heard she's on the exercise kick with the rest of the Ladies."

"She's working on it. Made me go through a bunch of boxes. I've got to cart all the junk over to the thrift store tomorrow."

"Did you find anything worth keeping?" Tara asked.

"A few things. A lot of it was my high school running stuff. I didn't remember how much stuff I had collected. T-shirts, ribbons, medals. There was even a pair of shoes. I don't know what the store will do with all that junk."

"Wouldn't you want to keep that stuff? It's kind of sentimental."

Ryan shrugged his shoulders. "I could barely look at it. It reminds me of the person I can't be anymore. It's like a knife twisting in my back."

"But you shouldn't throw it all away. In a few years, you might wish you had it."

"You sound like a self-help book." The romantic feeling disappeared as the grouch reared its head. He wanted to snap that he couldn't think about it now, but she kept talking.

"I went through something similar about four years ago. I was cut from the cheerleading squad and didn't know what to do. I bounced between a couple telemarketing jobs, but I ended up back home, still looking for a full-time job. I ran into Mark, and he recommended me for the job here."

"And you like this? The numbers, the details, the required perfection?"

"Seems like a stretch for me, huh?"

"Not a career choice I would have picked from my first impression. For you or for me." If he kept her talking about herself, he wouldn't have to contemplate his future for a while. He could listen to her voice and let his imagination go. His gaze traced the curve of her leg. "But it suits you."

"Me either, actually. But I started off answering the phones. Then as we got busier Leslie showed me some stuff and I enjoyed it. The numbers and organization made sense."

"What made you decide to get your degree?"

"I haven't decided yet."

"But the applications?"

"Yeah." She shrugged. "Leslie thinks I can pull it off. I'm not so sure. She needs the help though. I've been doing a few little things. She offered to help me with tuition if I would continue to work here after graduation. I shouldn't turn it down." She shifted to face him. Her legs pressed his and he blinked. There was no concentrating on anything she said now. "I was voted 'most likely to pose for a magazine spread' in high school." She laughed to herself. "Not going to happen now." She looked him over. "What were you voted in the mock elections?"

"Most likely to win on Jeopardy. Hasn't happened either." He absently rubbed his knee. "We certainly didn't turn out how everyone expected." He met her gaze and got lost in her blue eyes. Did anything else matter, but memorizing every gray fleck in them?

"There's still time for Jeopardy. I don't think I'll be in any magazines though."

"Maybe not the ones everyone thought back then. You could be in *Fortune* or *Money* magazine instead."

"Now there's a thought. It'd be a story for the class reunion." She tapped her finger against his chest, leaving burning imprints.

Her gaze slid over his face, resting finally on his lips. Ryan couldn't hold back anymore. He inched closer until he felt her sweet breath on his face. She licked her lips, and his last vestige of resistance melted. The space between them disappeared as his lips touched hers. At first tentatively, waiting for permission, then demanding because he needed her. Her hands slid over his shoulders and around his neck, revealing she was a more-than-willing participant. She pulled him toward her and he lost himself in the bliss.

Chapter Fifteen

Ryan loaded the records of his entire life into the back of his SUV. He was going to the Glendale thrift store to drop off all the medals and trophies as well as the junk his mother decided she could part with. If they didn't want the box of memorabilia and about a million T-shirts, his next stop would be the dump.

His mom had tried to talk him out of disposing of all the dust collectors, but he didn't want reminders of the life he couldn't have anymore. The dreams he had unfulfilled. He couldn't display them and didn't want to stumble across them in the basement.

His route took him past the Glendale athletic fields, circling past the tennis courts, the baseball field, and finally, the football stadium with the red ring around it where he'd logged his first miles. He swung his vehicle into the dirt parking lot and stared out the windshield.

He barely registered the radio playing his high school amp-up song. He must have tuned it to the local classic rock station by habit. The edgy singing egged him on. He'd worn out his cassette tape playing it over and over on his portable tape player to get his head in the zone.

A lone runner circled the track. A blond ponytail bouncing in the breeze from the lake beyond the field. He'd spent many a morning before school on the same route, hoping the extra mile or two would give him an edge in the next race. Old Coach Chambers had focused on the sprinters and throwers, because he knew how to condition them for football in the fall.

But Ryan, someone who wanted to run miles rather than meters, Coach didn't know what to do with. He'd throw out random mile numbers for Ryan to attain and no matter how bizarre, Ryan had pounded them out. Then he'd found a book on long distance running and made adjustments to his regimen, his diet, and his lifestyle. And one by one he'd collected the medals and trophies that filled the boxes in the back of his SUV.

The girl out there. What was her plan? She'd stopped at the fifty yard line and walked a tight circle, hands on her hips. Ryan glanced at the clock on the dashboard. Practice should be done by now. What was she still doing here? She circled around, then stopped at the starting line. She bent forward, then sprinted into the first curve.

He could feel the rush, the pump of adrenaline surging from nausea to speed, the moment when his lungs realized they needed to pace themselves and settle into a rhythm.

She came down the back stretch and hit the wall. Her stride broke apart. The smoothness of her movement jerked and tightened, but she dug harder. Her strides were stiffer instead of fluid, but her pace stayed steady through the finish. As her pace slowed, she turned back toward the high school, jogging. He expected to see her angle for the road for a cool down after a hard workout. She bee-lined straight for the building and disappeared inside.

Ryan rolled his eyes. Some things never changed. Coach Chambers hadn't imparted anything new about distance running and the necessity of cooling down after a workout.

Ryan better get over to the thrift shop before they closed. He threw the vehicle into reverse and backed out of his parking spot. The box of trophies clinked together from the movement of the SUV.

Maybe he didn't have to throw them away. Maybe the high school would want them. He didn't earn them all when he was a student, and those yellowed ribbons were hardly worth anything. But the medals for his marathons and the world championships, those might inspire someone — like the girl out there on the track — to train smarter, not harder.

Ryan drove across the lot to the front of the school. He lifted the gate on the back of the SUV and found the medals that might be inspiring to a young runner. Remind them Glendale wasn't too small for any dream. He stuffed them in his pocket and made for the stairs. The wide, flat steps had only acquired more layers of paint in the years since he'd graduated. He still remembered the rhythm needed to negotiate them without an awkward half-step, a gliding bound ascending from one surface to the next. He couldn't do it with a cane. He yanked open the heavy doors, getting the same buzz of adrenaline as the first day of ninth grade. A whole wide world had been open for him then. What options did he have now?

He signed in at the office, then headed into the hallway. The trophy cases were still inside the front door and brightly colored team pictures of impossibly young athletes filled the frames. Had he looked so young and bright? As he made his way toward the athletic director's office, he got his answer. The state championship trophy for track his senior year was still gathering cobwebs in the recesses of one of the glass cases. The picture had yellowed and his hair was too long, but the pure joy of his victory was plastered all over his face.

The locker room door burst open, broadcasting the pungent odor of sweat, socks, and teenage boys. The smell was probably etched into the tiles of the shower. The three boys jostled each other with baseball duffels hanging off their shoulders. Their jokes and jabs washed over him, and he was transported back to high school. He'd come so close to the dreams he'd seeded then.

He gripped his cane and hiked down the hallway. Those thoughts were better left unvisited.

As he continued to the athletic director's office, which was inexplicably on the other side of the building, he wondered if he would change anything knowing how quickly his body would succumb to the punishment. He would have kept running, probably leaving more on the track or the road than he had. Not taking any race as a step to another, but enjoying every footfall for its pure spirit.

He rapped his knuckles against the open office door, and the squat man who had wrangled the sports teams since there was a high school waved him in. His face shifted into a wide grin as soon as he recognized Ryan.

"Ryan Grant!" Mr. Tubbs boomed. "I heard you were back in the area." He stood and grabbed Ryan's hand in his two meaty ones. "Take a load off." He gestured to the gold vinyl chair beside the door.

Ryan sat, his knee screaming at him. He'd have to start planning his parking more strategically. *Park next to the entrance nearest what you need instead of by any door with a parking spot.*

"Good to see you again, Mr. Tubbs." Ryan let his gaze wander around the crammed office. Dusty red and gray pennants were tacked against team photos that hadn't been moved in fifteen years. The same carpet, the same paint scheme. The familiarity was oddly comforting. It helped him forget his life was upside down.

His eyes rested on a picture of himself, a black and white newspaper clipping as he crossed the tape where he earned one of the medals in his pocket. Mr. Tubbs had framed it.

"That was some moment, huh?" Mr. Tubbs tapped the photo.

The exhaustion, the exhilaration, the unbelievableness of that split-second flooded back to him. If he hadn't been sitting down, the memory would have knocked him over.

"Unbelievable." He shook his head to wave away the image. "I'm doing some cleaning, and I wondered if the school might be interested in these." He pulled the medals out of his pocket and passed them to Mr. Tubbs. "For the display cases." Ryan pointed his thumb over his shoulder to the miles he had traversed to get there.

Mr. Tubbs pushed his glasses onto his nose and picked up the red-and-green striped ribbon attached to the medal from the photo and rubbed his thumb over the inscription. "We watched these races on the big screen at Kelly's Bar. Bought the whole place a round when you broke the tape. Almost gave the missus a stroke when she saw the dent it made in our checking account, but she'd have done the same thing. Someone from little old Glendale at the World Championships." He shook his head as if he couldn't believe it. "You want to give these up?"

"Yeah, they're—" What could he say? Too painful? Like having his Achilles slashed every time he looked at them. Would Mr. Tubbs even understand when he only saw the triumph? "Maybe they'll inspire someone else."

Mr. Tubbs laid the medals reverently on his blotter. "That they will. Thank you for sharing them with us."

Ryan couldn't bear to listen as Mr. Tubbs reminisced. He didn't want to hear about the things he couldn't do anymore. Tubbs shuffled through the medals until his fingers grazed a bronze one in the shape of Michigan. He cradled it in his palm.

"Sometimes you see athletes work hard and do pretty well around here and then there's a kid like you. They have the extra drive, the extra talent to do something special. This race—" His lips tightened and his voice caught. "This race was when I knew you were going to do great things."

Ryan frowned at the bronze. A third place at his first state finals. His nerves had been so whacked, he'd thrown up in the warm up area. He'd run two laps before his stomach settled and the urge to heave dissipated.

"You looked so green on the starting line, I thought you were going to lose your lunch, but you held it together and came through the race strong. Kids need to see a hero overcome their nerves. It isn't always about winning these big races. It's about keeping your gut together." He closed the bronze in his fist. "I heard about your injury. What will you be doing now?"

Besides walking like an octogenarian for the rest of my life? Ryan scratched his nails into the rubber handle of his cane. "I haven't given it much thought. Until Monday I thought I would be running again in a few weeks, but now... I don't know."

Mr. Tubbs dangled the bronze between them. "If you've got some time on your hands," Mr. Tubbs said slowly, "Coach Chambers could use some help. He's got eight girls who thought track would be good conditioning for soccer and the football team has a chance at winning state next year."

Translation: Chambers hasn't got any time for the girls. "Are the girls any good?" Ryan asked. Why did he care? They wanted to play soccer not run track.

"I think there might be some potential there. Chambers wouldn't know, but one of the girls never seems to get winded. She's not breaking any speed records, but—" He tapped his finger by the Michigan medal. "She reminds me of you."

Everything inside Ryan snarled that being near the track team was a bad idea. How could he watch them run when he couldn't? Still he said, "I'll have to think about it" instead of flat out refusing.

"I'm afraid there isn't much time. There's only a month

left in the season. These girls could use your help now."

Ryan held his cane upright between his knees, smoothing his hand over the grip.

"I can't pay you this year. Nothing in the budget, but Chambers has been talking about cutting back. I may be able to work out something for you next year if you stick around."

"You really know how to sweeten the deal. I can't run with them. How am I supposed to coach them?"

"Chambers follows them on their runs in his station wagon eating a box of donuts. Whatever you can do wouldn't be worse." Mr. Tubbs rolled his eyes.

Ryan remembered the runner, circling the track. He didn't have the ability anymore, but he could share his wisdom and prevent the overtraining that caused his injury. But could he stand to be so close to his beloved sport without participating? It was the only way to get his running shoes on the track again, but he still couldn't say yes.

Chapter Sixteen

Charles swaggered out of his office, sliding his trench coat on his shoulders. "Any plans for this evening?"

"Just me and this computer," Tara said. He couldn't be leaving for the day. It was barely three-thirty. But if he wasn't, he was doing his own errands. Leaving was much more believable.

"The string bean dumped you, eh?"

Tara debated whether it was worth her energy to bite back at Charles or if she even had the energy to spare. She supposed 'string bean' referred to Ryan, though how Charles had surmised she and Ryan were anything, she didn't know. Even if he did know about their kiss, one kiss — no matter how earth-shattering — did not a relationship make. She narrowed her eyes. Her nerves were twisted so tightly they were snapping like the cords of a suspension bridge during an earthquake. Charles wasn't worth it.

It was Friday night. The office was open for four more hours, and he was cutting out early. They still had customers flowing in and a stack of returns to finish and send. Ryan was coming after they closed to do some work on the servers.

She hadn't had time to think about what their kiss meant. Was it only a kiss or something more? Did she want something more? Questions, questions, questions.

"I see," Charles said, jerking her out of her musing. "You dumped him." Charles tied the belt of his coat and picked up his briefcase. "Wanted a chance at something better." He winked. "I'll give you an audition later."

Tara rolled her eyes. She was too exhausted for his tired innuendos this afternoon. She hadn't had time for any of the pranks she and Ryan had talked about. Charles had almost pulled his weight today, but now he was bugging out early. She clenched her mouse and rolled her chair closer to her desk. *If you're going, just get.* Charles had rounded her desk and towered over her. She tugged on the lapel of her jacket, but she could still feel Charles's eyes crawling on her skin. It wasn't pleasant.

"Too bad I'm taken. At least for tonight. You were a couple hours late." He placed his hand on her desk and leaned over her shoulder. So close she could see the handprint of cologne he splashed on his chin. The fragrance choked her.

"You're just a pretty face with big boobs and neither of those is going to help you out much longer." His mouth was so close she could smell the unpasteurized cream from his coffee. The puffs of air tickling her face had her itching for disinfectant. "Your bookkeeping skills wouldn't last a day in the big city firms. Now if you'll excuse me, I have a date who knows how to use her assets." He tapped her on the shoulder, then squeezed it, before moving away and leaving behind a fog of cologne. He opened the door and left. Cool air tumbled in, dispelling his haze.

Tara stared at her computer screen, fighting the sting in her eyes. She was never going to overcome her lightweight image. Everywhere she went professionals would see her as the has-been cheerleader with nothing to recommend her but her implants. She looked down at her chest. If these were all she had to plan her future on, why should she kill herself trying to go college? No one but Leslie would ever take her seriously.

The next client arrived, and Tara tried to shove the thoughts of inadequacy aside, but they nipped at her anyway. First, she brought up the wrong file and almost verified someone else's social security number. Then she transposed numbers on their income, potentially costing them a hundred dollars in extra taxes. She pressed her thumb and forefinger against the bridge of her nose. The customer probably thought she had started her five o'clock somewhere a little early. She had to get a hold of herself. This was basically an EZ form. She could do this. She *had* to do this. Leslie trusted her. Giving the customer a weak smile, she tiptoed through the return, finally passing the refund sheet across the table for a signature.

Another two hours of customers, then she could lock the doors. She could survive. What she would do after closing… well, she would worry about it then.

The door opened and the wind caught the loose receipts in front of her computer. She flung herself across the desk as the papers floated away, knocking her cup of cold coffee over the side. The brown liquid splattered on the tile, but a masculine hand snatched the cup before it smashed on the tile.

Her eyes traveled up the hand, past the red windbreaker to meet Ryan's. She wanted to wrap her arms around his neck, snuggle into his chest and block out everything else. Their kiss flashed through her mind. Oh, she shouldn't think about it now. She'd never get back to work. It was too tempting to flee as quickly as Charles had.

Ryan juggled the cup and placed it on the edge of her desk. "Hey."

"What are you doing here?" She lifted herself off her desk and tugged her jacket back in place from where it had bunched up over her chest.

"Am I too early? To work on the server?" He shifted his

weight and tapped his cane against his toe. Was he nervous? "Is that still all right? I mean after…"

Tara stared at him for a moment, trying to collect her thoughts. His boyish awkwardness was rather cute. "No, I mean, yes. That would be great. It's been a long day." She didn't know what to do with her hands. Clasping them in front of her seemed school-girlish. Tucking them under her elbows, defensive. She grabbed her coffee cup and gestured for Ryan to follow her. "Thanks for coming. Charles was his usual self, then he cut out early. I've got at least half-a-dozen returns to finish and file tonight." She rubbed her hand over her forehead and smoothed some flyaways. "Probably should grab some paper towels for the spilled coffee too."

Ryan passed a look over the computer, then turned back to Tara. "I've got this. Go do what you need to do."

Tara hesitated, while Ryan shucked off his coat and slung it over the back of the chair by the server station. She should say something about last night, but what?

He reached out and touched her arm. "It's okay. Go finish your work. I'll be fine."

She nodded, blinking back tears. Ryan and Charles treated her so differently. Ryan so gentle, encouraging. Maybe there was one male who thought she wasn't a bunch of fluff. "Thanks," she murmured before hurrying back to her desk. She'd bury herself in her work and that would keep the tears at bay.

Chapter Seventeen

Tara ended the final appointment of the day and sank back into her chair. This was quite possibly the longest Friday ever, and she still wasn't done. She had to file the day's returns with the IRS and wait for the acceptance verification.

The hands on the clock had whizzed past nine o'clock. If she was lucky, she would be home by ten-thirty and could start forgetting this day ever happened.

She clicked the send button to file the returns with the IRS. The status bar and the estimated time remaining appeared. It claimed nine minutes, but it was never right. It would more likely be thirty or more. While she waited, she straightened her desk and pulled the files for the next day. She set Charles's files on his desk. No matter how much she disliked him, she needed his help with several returns. At first, he complained about her loading his desk with files every night, but now he seemed as grateful as he was capable. She liked being more familiar with the client's history so she didn't miss any obvious deductions or credits.

The send/receive status was still crunching along when she finished, so she straightened up the toys and watered the plants before she tackled the mountain of backed up filing. As she retrieved the watering can from under the sink in the break room, she asked Ryan how things were going. He was paging through lists of file names on the screen.

"Not bad. I'm clearing out the temporary files bogging things down. It should speed things up." He let go of the mouse and leaned back in his chair.

She sighed. "Sounds good. Hopefully it will stop Charles from complaining about the computer system." She might be able to close up and sink into her bed within the hour. The computer chimed the transaction was complete. It had taken forty-five minutes. She clicked 'okay' to view the rejected returns. Only one. *Thank goodness.* Hopefully, it'd be a quick fix. She could resend it and get out of here.

She matched the number to her list of returns and pulled the file. It was one of Charles's. She groaned. Unless it was an easy error, she wouldn't be able to resend it tonight. Charles would have to go over it in the morning. She pulled out the paper file from her stack and started with verifying the social security numbers.

Ah, there was the problem. The last two numbers of the spouse's number had been transposed. She could correct it and resend and still make her appointment with her bed. She made the changes to the computer file and then went to make a note on the printed file about the error and the resend.

This year's return was not on the top of the file. Maybe Charles put it on the bottom. She checked. Not there either. What would Charles have done with it? He could simply have forgotten to print one out. Did he stick it in the wrong file? Nope. A quick glance through the rest of the folders didn't reveal it, but none of them had the most recent return in them. It was hard to believe he was doing that much work. He must hunker down and plow through the returns while she skipped around town on his errands.

But what was he doing with the returns? He could be

giving that copy to the client. She shrugged. It didn't matter. She'd have to print out new ones, which she might as well do now while she was thinking about it. She clicked print on the current file, then accessed the rest of them and sent them to the printer as well. As she collected the sheets spewing from the printer, she realized he probably did the same thing for every return he did. She'd have to check them all.

She groaned. So much for getting home at a decent hour. She started to make a list of the files she'd need, cursing Charles with every name she added to it. After finishing the list, she kicked off her shoes. Then she remembered something Leslie had said about being able to print multiple files at once. Tara selected the files and hit print. Paper shot out of the printer and landed in the tray. All she had left was stapling and shoving them in the appropriate folders. She made a quick trip to the bathroom and returned to find the papers tumbling from the printer and spewing to the floor like a tornado propelled them.

Crap. Now she'd have to match the pages of each return. She'd be here until midnight.

She hitched up her skirt and knelt on the floor to sort the papers. She had finagled three full returns out of the whirlwind when she noticed something funny about them. All the addresses for the refund were using post office boxes. A few people did that, but definitely not all of them. She shifted to plant her butt on the floor and studied the returns. The post office box was an hour away. Few people in town would drive out of town for their mail, and she knew these three households didn't. She stared at the papers in front of her. The box numbers were all the same. Wasn't there a lawyer who put estates in an escrow account? That could explain it. She scrambled through the papers and found three more with the same address.

There was no way that was right. These three individuals didn't even speak to each other let alone share a post office box an hour away. And they weren't dead.

Tara found the second page of the remaining 1040s. Each one listed the same mailing address.

Her heart pounded in her chest. This was a big error. Charles must not have updated it. Her hands shook as she laid the papers down in front of her.

No, that wasn't right. The address information pulled directly from their client files. They shouldn't have to update anything unless the client had moved.

So what was going on? It couldn't be a mistake. She grabbed one of the returns and checked the name. Cliff Simons. Didn't he die two years before? Tara scrambled for the files on her desk and searched for Cliff's. Second to last, of course, but she weaseled it out and flipped the file open. The last return was two years old. By the staple at the top of the last refund was a scrap of pink paper. The paper they used to note the client's file was closed because he or she had died. That notice had been torn out.

Charles had filed a return for a dead person? Then she gasped. Charles had filed a return using a dead person's social security number. The check would go to the P.O. box; Charles would pick it up, and sail away with some extra cash. Just a little identity theft and a dash of tax fraud.

Tara crouched back on the floor by the other returns. Would he do something so easily found out? He had done little to hide his tracks.

He wasn't the sharpest saw in the shed. Most of these refunds were only a few hundred dollars, not enough to draw the IRS's attention, but altogether, it was quite a sum of money. Of course, if he hadn't transposed the numbers, she wouldn't have found the theft until the IRS came knocking on the door. He would be sunning himself on a beach somewhere by then.

What could she do? He hadn't actually stolen any money yet. None of the refunds would have arrived at the P.O. box.

She did, however, have proof of fraud. This would be a way to get rid of him.

She started to organize the returns, mentally preparing a list of what she would need to present the police. Then she noticed one other number was the same on all the returns.

She slumped back against the side of the printer station.

Crap.

She obviously wasn't cut out for this. Charles had been right.

Chapter Eighteen

Tara slouched against the printer stand in front of a splash of papers when Ryan sauntered out of the server room. He rolled the tight muscles in his shoulders and heard several satisfying pops. He tapped on the wall with his knuckle to get her attention and Tara flinched. Her eyes flared and she gasped for air. Thankfully, she recognized him right away. He was afraid she might scream.

"I can't believe this." Her voice trembled. *Was she close to tears?*

Ryan cocked his head to see what the papers on the floor were. Tax returns, he guessed from the 1040 on the top, but beyond that he didn't see the problem. "What's going on?"

Tara shook her head. Her blond hair was slipping from its tight knot. Tendrils fell around her face, but he realized they hadn't come naturally loose. She had been digging her fingers through it. "I made a huge mistake."

"It can't be that bad." He pulled her to her feet and wrapped her in his arms. Her breath came in sharp gasps. "It will be all right. Breathe for a minute." He crowded her close to his chest, whispering calming words into her ear. He trailed his fingertips up and down her back. Eventually, her breathing eased enough that she could form a full sentence.

"I think Charles is trying to defraud the IRS." Her words spilled out like water from a faulty fire hydrant. "And he's going to pin it on me."

"What? How?" He wanted to wrap his arms around her and protect her from everything related to Charles. His fancy cream cheese, his cheap innuendos, and his smarmy grin. She was working so hard, but Charles did nothing but make it more difficult. Ryan eased her over to the waiting area and encouraged her to sit. He perched on the seat next to her and stretched his bad leg out.

Tara waved her hand as if trying to clear the dust away and read an explanation of the situation. She jumped from her seat and dashed to her desk. She grabbed a folder with papers stuffed haphazardly inside and one of the stacks of paper from the floor. When she sat and opened the folder on her lap, the papers fluttered to the ground. Ryan reached to the carpet to scoop up the ones he could reach. A quick scan told him it was a list of numbers and dates and codes, but nothing made sense to him.

"What are these?" He handed the sheets to Tara. She shuffled them together, but the papers wouldn't cooperate. They caught each other's edges and rolled the wrong way.

"The e-file reports. I file the returns at the end of the day and get this report once they've all gone through. It tells me if anything has been rejected and why. I checked the errors and double-checked those returns, but then tonight there was one with an incorrect social security number. I went to verify them with the original return and found this." She switched to the pile of papers from the floor and held out two pages.

"What was wrong with it?"

"Nothing at first. These returns were filed and accepted by the IRS, but the file should be closed."

"Closed, what does that mean?" Ryan eased around in

his seat so he could see Tara's face. Tension etched lines along her jaw. He itched to smooth away the marks on her skin. She blinked rapidly. Was she going to cry? Tears? He didn't think he could handle those. Besides this couldn't be that bad. It was someone's taxes. For all he knew, they could send in a corrected return and it would all be fixed. Well, that and a few interest payments if they owed the government money.

"We close a file when a client dies." Confidence built in Tara's voice as she explained their procedures. She knew her stuff, and she wouldn't make a mistake like this. The way she zipped through his, it was obvious she understood the implications. Her boss wouldn't be encouraging her to get the degree if she didn't pay attention to details. "Most people don't need to file a return more than for the year they died, unless they have huge estates, which isn't any of our clients. We have a lot of multi-generation families with similar names or even the same names, so we lock the file so we don't accidentally do something like this."

"File a return for a dead person?" Every word Tara spoke made Ryan more glad he didn't do his own taxes. There was too much complication to keep it all straight.

"Yes. If this was the only one, I would think it was a mistake and call the IRS and clear it up, nightmare that that would be. But—" She turned to the next paper and the next, indicating lines on each one. "There are several of them. All posting returns with refunds in the form of checks instead of direct deposit and all going to the same P.O. box."

"So it's not a mistake." Ryan knew he was being Captain Obvious, but he didn't know what else to say. He'd never actually witnessed fraud before.

"It's identity theft. The IRS went after a bunch of tax preparers last year for it. But that's not the worst of it. See this code?" Tara pressed a manicured nail against the last column on the page. "This is the tax preparer code. It's mine."

"Doesn't the whole office use the same one?"

"No. They are individualized. I created one for Charles, since his old one was expired. See. It's here." She pointed to another line. "This return is completely legitimate."

"He's trying to frame you." A ball of ice sunk in Ryan's stomach. He finally understood what had Tara so agitated. This was her career on the line. Her confidence in her ability was shaky already. This knocked out three legs of the overloaded table. He'd like to take an opportune swipe at Charles's shins with his cane.

"I think so." She flicked the edges of the papers with her fingernail. "I checked them all. My ID is on every single one of the fraudulent returns."

"Did he think you wouldn't figure it out?" Ryan reached for the folder and flipped it open. He scanned the papers, but didn't see anything that would do any good. Granted, he had no idea what he was looking at.

"Probably. He's more interested in the ounces of saline in my chest than anything between my ears." Tara pushed a loose strand of hair behind her ear. "He said as much before he left today."

How Charles could ignore Tara's competence, Ryan didn't know. Actually, in the few moments he'd observed Charles, he did. Charles didn't see any woman as more than her measurements.

In Ryan's estimation, Tara had phenomenal measurements and they had drawn him to her initially, but after spending time with her, he knew she had so much more to offer. Her intelligence and quick thinking were keeping this place afloat, despite what she thought. Charles wasn't doing a thing to help her. If Ryan committed to staying in Carterville permanently, he'd consider much more with Tara than their occasional dinner and coffee.

"So what are you going to do?" he asked Tara.

"That's just it. I don't know. How can I prove I didn't prepare these returns? They have my name on them. I'm responsible for them. Leslie's only been out of the office for five days, and I've already destroyed her company. The IRS will eat me alive and completely ruin Leslie's reputation." She slumped forward, resting her head on her hands and her elbows on her knees. Her shoulders shook and he heard the tiniest sniff. She was crying, holding it in hard, but crying nonetheless. He had to stop the tears now.

"There's got to be a way around this. Something to prove you weren't the one who prepared the returns. What about at what computer the return was prepared?" He suggested, grasping for anything that might help Tara and end the droplets of water that trailed down her cheeks.

She looked up at him and eyes widened. "Oh my goodness. I hadn't even thought of that. No wonder he thought he could pin this on me. It's obvious I can't think my way out of a paper bag."

It was ridiculous how easy the wrong person could shake someone's confidence. Charles knew exactly which buttons to push for the desired result. What a worthless piece of carbon. "Don't beat yourself up. You discovered it tonight. He's barely been at it a week. That's pretty quick, in my opinion. We have to make sure we have all our ducks in a row before you present this information to the authorities."

"We?" Tara squeaked and the tears stopped.

"You bet. I've got your back. There's got to be a computer trail, and we are going to find it." He'd scour that computer system and make sure Charles took the fall for his scheme. If only to keep any more tears from Tara's eyes.

"Why are you helping me?" Tara sniffed and rubbed her nose with the back of her hand.

"Why shouldn't I?" Ryan wrapped his arm around her shoulders and squeezed her to his chest. He pressed his lips to her temple. He'd do everything he could to help her. That was what you did for people you cared about, right? "You deserve it."

Chapter Nineteen

Tara's cell phone vibrated against her hip. She wiggled the phone out of her skirt pocket and scowled at the display. "Charles," she said with a huff. "What's his problem? Hot date fizzled and looking for a booty call?"

"Don't answer it," Ryan said. "Whatever his problem is, it can wait until Monday."

Tara wrapped her hand around the phone and nodded. "You're right." She slipped the phone back in her pocket. "Where should we start?"

"I'll get a backup started, so that he can't go back in and change anything when he comes back to work."

"I'm not letting him back through the door. I'm calling Leslie in the morning to see if I can find someone else to help."

"I don't see why you don't do this yourself."

"Isn't it obvious? I've only had Charles here a week, and he's committed identity theft and fraud. How badly would I screw up if I was doing everything on my own?"

"Well, you wouldn't have Charles trying to put you in prison." Ryan was cut off by the buzzing of Tara's phone. She glanced at the display, snarled something atrocious and shoved it back in her pocket. "Charles again?"

Tara didn't have to answer because the office phone rang. Tara thanked God one more time for the invention of caller ID. It was after hours, and she would only answer the phone if it was important. But when Hammerin' Hank's Towing Service's number appeared on the display, curiosity got the better of her. Hank wouldn't be calling her this late unless he was towing her car. She craned her neck to see the rust bucket still corroding in the parking lot. She picked up the phone. "Hey, Hank, whatcha need?" Her voice sounded surprisingly more cheerful than she felt.

"Can you get this idiot out of his car?" Hank bellowed into her ear.

She had a bad feeling about which idiot Hank was referring to, but asked for confirmation anyway. "Who are you talking about?"

"I'm out by Bubba's and that fancy-pants you work with hit a deer and put his swanky car in the ditch. And now Bubba's out here, scoping out the deer carcass and Mr. Fancy-pants won't get out of his blasted car with that Neanderthal waving his shotgun around."

If Hank was calling Bubba a caveman, Bubba had to be putting on a big and horrifying show. It was tempting to tell Hank to let Bubba shoot Charles. She didn't want to lift a hangnail to help him out. Frustration and exhaustion warred with each other. "I can't help you."

"C'mon, Tara. I've got three calls to get to tonight, and Angelina is home with the twins who have been puking their guts out since dawn. She's gonna break my neck if I don't get home before midnight. And this moron won't get out of his car."

"Tow the car with him in it. Park him at Dave's garage, and he can cool his heels there until he decides to get out of the car." Ryan was nodding. Tara took that to mean he liked the plan. Her confidence boosted a smidge.

"I can't tow a car with a person in it. My insurance would get yanked, then I'd be up a crick for sure."

"Then leave him there. I don't care." Tara rubbed her forehead. She didn't want to deal with this now. She'd rather find a way to save her own butt than rescue Charles's. Ryan raised his finger and mouthed something to her, but she couldn't make out his message.

"Just talk to him. He'll listen to you," Hank said.

Tara squeezed her eyes shut and murmured the words, "Put the moron on the phone." Then she realized, she didn't actually say anything. She repeated the words loud enough for Hank to hear.

"I can't. He won't even open his window." Tara picked up a pencil from her desk and crammed the eraser end down on to a manila folder. She was surprised Hank hadn't already broken the window and yanked Charles through the jagged glass. She raised her eyebrows. The idea had appeal. Shredding Charles's freshly dry-cleaned suit on the shards... Then Hank asked, "Can you call him?" shaking her out of her revelry.

"Hank!"

"My life's on the line here. You know Angelina. She'll bust my chops if I don't get home."

Tara knew he had a point. Few people could scare Hank, but his wife led him around on a leash. They had three sets of twins and each one got a bigger dash of mischief in their DNA. On their best behavior, they made Boppy seem like the teacher's pet. Sick? Tara shuddered at the thought. "Okay, I'll call him. For Angelina. And next time my car takes a dump, you're there in five minutes."

"You got it. It'll be a freebie," Hank promised and hung up.

Tara dropped the handset back into the receiver. She jammed her hands on her hips, her head filling with the things she'd rather do than dial Charles's number. Ryan stood and picked up his cane.

"If we pick him up, we'll know where he is and be able to keep an eye on him."

She turned to look at Ryan. "Pick him up? I don't want to call him on the phone, let alone see his smarmy face right now." She snarled at her phone. "Best get it over with." She pressed it to her ear. The tones buzzed, only to be followed by a canned voice directing her to leave a message. "He probably burned out his battery." She slumped against the edge of her desk. "I don't want to go out there."

Ryan came over to her and put his arm around her shoulders. "Think of it this way. Keep your friends close and your enemies closer."

"I don't want to keep him within a baseball throw." She slid a skeptical glance to the side, but leaned into his muscled chest anyway. No matter what she said, having Ryan here helped.

"We pick him up. His car is totaled, so he can't skip town. Once we figure out how to prove the fraud, we can have him arrested. He won't get away with this."

"It won't be that simple." Tara shook her head, but liked Ryan's thought process. If Charles could leave, they'd never catch him. He had scammed enough money to skip the country — once the checks came in. Nothing had been delivered to his P.O. Box yet. They had a little time.

"It just might." Ryan squeezed her closer.

Chapter Twenty

They found Charles's car angled in the ditch with the rear tires about four inches off the ground. Hank paced behind his truck with his cell phone plastered to his ear; his rotund figure defied gravity. Bubba had made quick work of the deer and disappeared from the scene, leaving a pile of entrails about two feet from the driver's side door of the swanky car.

Hank snapped his phone into the clip on his belt as Ryan and Tara climbed out of her sedan. It had seen the back of Hank's tow truck for more miles than she'd dared to count. That her car wasn't being hooked to the truck was the only thing going in her favor tonight.

He gestured helplessly toward Charles. "I think Bubba scared the crap out of him."

"Doesn't surprise me. Charles probably thinks his filet mignon appears on his plate by magic." Tara flexed her shoulders and marched over to Charles's car. Ryan took the straps Hank handed him and started untangling them, while Hank prepared to winch the car onto the flatbed.

Tara sidestepped around the remains of the deer and inched her way down the weed-entangled ditch. Her heels caught on the dried grass, but she righted herself before she face-planted into Charles's window. Charles was hunched into the seat, his head barely visible above the upturned collar of his coat. He must have glimpsed her movement out of the corner of his eye because the locks clicked, reiterating that the vehicle was his little foxhole in the rural wilds.

After all the characters he had met with tonight, the most dangerous to him was rapping on his window, Tara thought as she pounded her palm against the tinted glass. She took special glee in watching him flinch. When he recognized her, he unlocked the door, then scrambled out. His foot caught the edge of entrails and he slipped into the weeds. He frantically scrubbed his heel against the grass, before dashing across the road into the shotgun seat of her car. He pressed the lock button, only to have the mechanism pop open after every try.

"I always figured if someone stole the car, they deserved what they got," she called as she climbed out of the ditch.

"Get me out of here," Charles called back, fumbling for his seatbelt and snapping it in place.

If she didn't think what Bubba did to the deer was too good for Charles, she would have laughed hysterically. She'd never seen a grown man act like a frightened four-year-old.

Hank clapped her on the shoulder so hard her knees buckled. "Thanks," he grunted. "It'll take me a few minutes to get the car hooked up. Where should I take it?"

"Keep it at your yard. I'm taking him to the Lilac Bower."

"The Bower? Don't you think he's had enough for one night?" Hank raised an eyebrow.

"Not even close."

"Okey-dokey." Hank climbed in the cab of his truck and shifted into reverse. The lights on the truck flashed.

Tara shivered and shoved her hands deeper into her pockets. An April night still wasn't warm enough to stand out in the cold for more than a few minutes, but if risking pneumonia meant avoiding Charles's presence for another five minutes, she welcomed her chances with the cold.

Hank loaded the car onto the trailer with practiced efficiency. They were quickly on their way back into town. Ryan had crammed himself into the seat behind Charles while Tara drove and Hank followed with the tow truck.

Charles watched Hank's lights in the side mirror vigilantly. When Hank turned off to his garage, Charles jumped in his seat. "Where'd he go with my car?"

Tara wanted to remind him if he had actually talked to Hank, he would know, but having words with him, civil or otherwise, was not among her talents tonight. She kept her eyes on the road and her hands on the wheel. It was all she could do to not sideswipe the passenger side of the vehicle into each telephone pole she passed. Ryan stepped in and explained Hank would have a certified mechanic look at the damage in the morning.

"How'd you end up out by Bubba's?" Tara asked as she adjusted the heater vents, so the warm air blasted against her frozen hands. She didn't care if Charles was shivering.

Charles pursed his lips and shook his head. "I must have taken a wrong turn."

Bubba was known for stealing the street signs and recycling them for scrap metal. It made sense. And that was all he would say about it. Tara jammed the shifter into park after she finally pulled into the Lilac Bower parking lot. The whole ride, she had been counting the minutes until she could rid herself of his presence. Even at this late hour, lights twinkled around the porch, giving the bed and breakfast a warm, non-redneck feel, somewhat more suited to Charles's tastes.

Charles seemed to be more at ease with this neighborhood. He climbed out of the car, straightened the collar of his coat and smoothed his hair. "What's this place?"

"It's a bed and breakfast. You can stay here until your car gets fixed." *Or until you get hauled off to the pokey*, she thought. She added out loud, "It's walking distance to the office."

Charles surveyed the wrap-around porch lit by old-fashioned lanterns. "Isn't there a Hilton in town?"

"There's a place with a pool, but it's in Glendale. It's after eleven, and I'm not driving all the way over there." Tara marched up the sidewalk leading to the front door. He could follow her or not. If he didn't, she would at least let Minnie know who was sleeping on her lawn. If her night was looking up, perhaps Charles would be arrested for vagrancy.

"Do you think Minnie's still up?" Ryan asked, hop-stepping to keep up with her.

"Of course, she is. She always watches those shop-at-home channels until midnight. She says the best deals are after 11:30." Tara climbed the stairs and punched the doorbell. A pleasant chime played.

A few moments later, Minnie arrived at the door with the phone pressed to her ear and a remote tucked under her arm. She waved for them to come in, but continued her conversation with the customer service representative. "No. No. The other one. With the feathers. Yes. Does it come with the instruction video? Oh good."

Tara entered the foyer, followed by Ryan. Charles reluctantly climbed the steps of the porch as if the Lilac Bower was only slightly better than Bubba's Demolition. Ryan closed the door behind them.

Minnie ended the phone call and placed the handset on a gunmetal-gray, silk runner on a side table.

"Good evening, Tara, Ryan. How can I help you?"

Tara started to explain about the deer, the Mercedes, and Charles needing a room, but Minnie's gaze swung to Ryan.

"So," Minnie said, looking from Tara to Ryan and back. She wiggled her eyebrows. Tara couldn't miss Minnie's insinuation, but a rendezvous was not in the cards for the evening. More likely she'd be studying spreadsheets until her eyes resembled knots in the bark of a tree.

Tara shook her head. "Charles needs a room for the night.

He hit a deer out by Bubba's."

"What was he doing out there at night? Doesn't he know?" Minnie turned to Charles who had barely ventured over the threshold, a look of mild disgust plastered his face.

So the Bower wasn't up to his standards after all. Tara sighed. There really was no pleasing him.

Minnie's forehead crinkled, revealing wrinkles not evident before. "I've seen you somewhere."

Charles didn't say anything, nor would he make eye contact. He crossed his arms over his chest and examined the crown molding.

"Charles, Charles," Minnie repeated. "Charles..." Then she hissed. "Chuck!" She spit on the rug by his feet. Charles jumped and Tara gasped. While Minnie was plain-spoken in her opinions, Tara had never seen her react with such disgust or violence.

"No one calls me that anymore," Charles sniffed, refusing to meet Minnie's piercing stare.

"Well, I can't say what they should call you." Minnie went off on a mumbled tirade Tara was glad she couldn't entirely understand. It contained several words best contained in a losing team's locker room.

Why does 'Chuck' ring a bell? The way Minnie snarled it brought stories to the forefront of her mind. Chuck. Leslie had worked with a Chuck, had a promotion stolen by a Chuck, been fired by a Chuck. Then she gasped, "Oh no!"

Horror gripped her and the room started to spin. She tried to turn herself to keep up with it. She couldn't have summoned this same slimy Chuck to Carterville.

"What's going on?" Ryan asked, grabbing hold of Tara's arm to arrest her spinning. She clutched the solidness of his arm, desperate for something to keep the rest of her life from tipping into the gutter. The room wobbled, then righted.

Minnie muttered something that sounded like a hex, possibly involving infected boils.

Tara looked up into Ryan's eyes, focusing on the flecks of gray amid the blue as if they were the only anchor keeping her from washing away on a sea of her own stupidity.

"Chuck. Chuck. The hair. It's different. And no earring. How could I have been so stupid?" Tara cried, burying her face in her hands. She had seen him when he dropped by after Leslie opened the office. How had she not recognized him? "This is absolutely horrible." Her voice trailed off into a wail.

"Who is Chuck?" Ryan asked again. He gripped her arms and kept her face focused on his. Tara's eyes filled with tears. She couldn't help it. She screwed everything up. She should have 'failure' stamped on her forehead. She couldn't even look up a phone number in an address book. Add to that identity theft and tax fraud. Chuck had probably swiped all the sticky notes too. She should quit right now.

"I might as well have burned down the building." Tara sniffed, waving helplessly at Chuck. "I couldn't have done anything worse."

Ryan pulled her into his arms. Even though her mind swirled with horror and frustration, she found refuge. With his arms steadying her, she could almost believe everything good in her life hadn't been flushed down the toilet.

"He's the sleezeball who got Leslie fired from her job after she came here." Minnie jabbed her finger at Chuck. Chuck jerked backward as if she'd electrocuted him. Maybe Minnie's hex was stronger than she thought. "How could you even think she would want you here?"

"It was my mistake, Minnie," Tara cried. "I called him. I was in too much of a hurry and got the wrong Charlie."

"Leslie's always had a soft spot for me." Chuck shrugged his shoulders. "I'm the reason she got as far as she did in the company."

"Baloney. You rode her coat-tails as far as you could and slept your way up the rest of the time. You are a slimy, sleazy butthead. I can't believe I was afraid you would leave."

Minnie snorted. "You can say that again."

"Leslie thought you were her friend and you stabbed her in the back. She told me all about it," Tara shouted. Her fury built and she inched toward him. She wouldn't let him get away with any of it. He wouldn't hurt Leslie's company. He wouldn't pin his fraud on her. And he wouldn't leave town unless it was in the back of an IRS paddy-wagon. Well, they probably didn't have paddy-wagons, but he'd surely get some new bracelets. She jabbed her finger at him. "I should have left you out at Bubba's."

"Hey." Chuck wagged his finger as he inched behind Minnie who looked as if she could use his tie as a deadly weapon. "Your message begged me to come. I'm doing you a huge favor."

"But I didn't know who you were. If I had, I wouldn't have let you and your sorry cream cheese into our office, let alone cross the city limits."

Leslie had trusted her. That was the worst part of it. How badly would Leslie be disappointed? She was the first one to think Tara was anything more than her bra size. And here she had proven she was a failure. She swayed back into Ryan.

"What are we going to do about him?" Ryan asked. He squeezed her arm.

How could he still believe in her? "He stays here. Sorry, Minnie. Can I talk to you for a second?"

When Minnie nodded, Tara pulled her down the hallway out of earshot of Ryan and Chuck. In frantic whispers, she explained the fraudulent tax returns Chuck had filed and how they didn't want him to leave town until they could prove he did it.

"It's all right. He won't be going anywhere until the police slap the cuffs on him. And by then he'll be begging them to take him away." Minnie gave Tara a hug and whispered in her ear, "I don't hold grudges — I get revenge. And I have friends who will hide the body." Minnie's eyes narrowed as her gaze swung to Chuck. "I've got just the room for you, buster." She grabbed his arm and marched him up the stairs.

"Minnie doesn't have any rooms with electroshock equipment, does she?" Ryan asked, his voice low on her ear.

"Not on my last tour, but she is still working on upgrades." Minnie and Chuck disappeared at the top of the staircase. "There is one room she claims is haunted." Tara turned to Ryan. "I have to tell Leslie about this. He is the last person she would have wanted sitting in her office, using her computer, accessing her files..." Tara gasped. "Using all her information to commit identity fraud. I have to make this right." She dashed for the door.

"Hey, wait up! Where are you going?" Ryan hobbled after her.

"I have to confess to Leslie and then get to work. He isn't going to get away with this, even if Leslie fires me. I'm going to make sure he goes to jail," she called as she flew down the steps.

"Wait for me," Ryan called as she yanked her car door open. It made a menacing creak.

"You don't need to come. I screwed this up myself, I have to fix it myself."

"I promised I would help." He walked awkwardly down the sidewalk and eased into the passenger seat.

Tara shook her head. She was so focused on finding out how Chuck had sabotaged them, she could hardly think of anything else. "Right. Sorry." She started the engine, but waited to shift into reverse until Ryan's seatbelt was firmly in place.

They drove the streets in silence. Tara's mind was jumping between rehearsing a speech for Leslie and finding the incriminating evidence against Chuck. She didn't notice Ryan hadn't said a word until she nailed the pothole in the office parking lot and heard him grunt.

"I'm sorry I dragged you into all this." She spared him a quick glance before swinging her car into a parking spot directly in front of the office.

Ryan unsnapped his seatbelt and turned toward her. His windbreaker whistled against the seat. "My offer stands. I want to help."

"You don't have to." She pulled the keys out of the ignition and wrapped them in her palm. "It's my mistake. I have to fix it."

"I know I don't have to." Ryan brushed his fingers across her cheek. "I want to."

Tara blinked rapidly. She was turning into a watering pot tonight. Her eyeliner had to be raccoon-like smears around her eyes. A shoulder to lean on, to give support was so tempting. She could give in tonight and allow him to help. Tomorrow, she could gather her wits and stand on her feet. Talking it all out with Ryan would help. She willed the tears back and let the oxygen into her lungs, then pushed the carbon dioxide out. Slow and steady. "Thank you." She reached for the door handle, then stopped and swung back to Ryan. "Why?"

She could barely see his face in the silhouette of the streetlight. His mouth moved, but no sound came out.

"We just met. You don't know me from Adam, and now you are willing to help me catch someone guilty of identity fraud. What's in it for you?"

His eyes softened and he searched hers. "I need a distraction. Something to get my mind off not being able to run. To prove I'm useful for something."

Tara slumped in her seat, then tucked her keys in her pocket, and reached for the door. He was here for 'the computer, not for her. Their kiss last night meant nothing now, if it ever did. Her incompetence had soured the relationship before it had started. Time to lock down her heart, so she didn't risk anymore hurt tonight. She had been battered and bruised in every aspect of her life. She climbed out of the car and headed for the door, more aware than she wished of Ryan's presence. Her hands shook as she worked the key in the lock.

Ryan followed her to the door as she fumbled with the keys. He laid his hand over hers. "Do you have to do this now? Why not go home and get some rest? Minnie won't let Chuck go anywhere. Come back in the morning."

Tara shook her head. She'd never sleep and she needed the distraction of work. "I can't. I want to call Leslie first thing in the morning and I need to have something about where the investigation is going to prove I'm not a complete idiot."

Chapter Twenty-One

Ryan stretched back in his seat. The chair protested with a rancorous crack. He sat forward and pressed his palms to his eyes. It was long past being a good idea to switch from contacts to glasses, but his glasses were in the case at his mom's. He wouldn't quit working if Tara didn't, although a shot of caffeine should have been ordered a half hour before. He blinked rapidly, hoping there was enough moisture in his eyelids to unstick the lenses from his eyeballs.

Tara crouched by her desk, thumbing through the files in the lower drawer. She'd shed her jacket and her hair tumbled from the neat twist-up thingy it had been earlier. His gaze traveled slowly down her back to the enticing curve where her skirt stretched over her bottom. His thoughts strayed to what those curves would feel like pressed into his lap. He shifted in his seat. Parts of him weren't as tired as others.

He stood with the intention of waking up the rest of his body with a break. As soon as he gained his feet, his body slipped sideways, and he slammed his cheekbone into the doorjamb.

Stupid knee. When would it be strong enough to hold his

weight without concentration? Gripping the door jamb, he flexed his leg, easing the stiffness that had accumulated in the last hour.

He reached around the table and grabbed his cane, remembering to shift it to his right hand like the physical therapist had pounded into his head. Keeping track of the movements he could and couldn't do was harder than working through the strength exercises. Bend this way, not that. Turn this way, not that. But then he was used to physical exertion. He'd been blessed with naturally good running form, so he rarely had to do conditioning to correct inefficiencies in his movement.

Gripping his cane, he made his way down the hallway from the break room. Tara shifted and her blouse slipped away from her skirt, revealing the creamy skin underneath. She slapped a manila folder on the pile next to the drawer and raised herself to her feet. She bent to pick up the rest of the pile and her shirt gaped higher. Along her side, the silky skin transformed to twisted and blotchy scar tissue.

Tara twisted toward him. "How's it going on your end?" She brushed a loose hair out of her face. "I think I've found all the paper files Chuck accessed."

Ryan stared at her side. He couldn't pull his gaze away, no matter how rude it felt.

"Oh." She half-smiled. He knew she was trying to shrug it off like it was no big deal. She tugged her blouse down and worked to adjust the band of her skirt to overlap.

He put his hand over hers to stop the movement, tracing his fingertips over the bunched ridges. Her stomach muscles trembled under his touch. "How did this happen?"

She straightened and gripped the edge of her shirt, inching it up to bare more of the ravaged flesh. "One car accident and more plastic surgeries and skin grafts than I can count."

Ryan let out a long breath. "Makes the marble-sized

incisions on my knee seem like mosquito bites."

He leaned his forehead against hers, smoothing his thumb over the ridges at her side. His stomach squirmed at the thought of the pain she had suffered. He'd intended their relationship to be a simple flirtation, something to distract him during his recovery, but after the last couple days, he knew he cared more deeply for her. If he wasn't careful, he would hurt her when he left. But he was very much in danger of hurting himself. His baloney earlier about the computer being a distraction was just a cover. She was the reason he was willing to hunch over a keyboard and scan lines of code.

"It certainly wasn't fun." Her voice was barely above a whisper.

"I didn't mean to look," he added, but he couldn't stop caressing her skin. The warmth of her body traversed his fingertips. Sliding them higher was irresistible.

She dropped the edge of her shirt and tapped him on the chin. "I don't believe that for a second."

Ryan tipped his head toward hers, lingering in the sweet blue of her eyes. "How about I don't mean to stop?"

Under his hand, her chest trembled in a silent laugh. "Now that sounds like a man."

"That sounds like your man." The words tripped out before Ryan even thought about the implications. They felt right, but they also scared the crap out of him. He shouldn't commit to anyone or anything besides his recovery. It wasn't fair.

"What's that supposed to mean?" She tilted her head back to look him in the eye. Ryan knew he didn't have an answer. He lowered his lips to hers, dismissing the warning that he was committing to something he couldn't put into words. He was too tired to deal with it now. He needed her. Her arms slid around him, and her fingers pressed into the muscles at his back. He pulled her tighter, crushing her against his chest, driving all thoughts of releasing her out of his reach.

His hands slid under her blouse, mapping the extent of her scars into his memory. They stretched from waist to bra. As much as he wanted to, he didn't test the skin under the satiny fabric. The temptation threatened, but his balance didn't cooperate. He stumbled backward, landing with a hard thump on his butt. He managed to cradle Tara, so she crashed into his chest rather than tumbling to the tile.

"Guess I'm not used to my weak leg yet." He laughed as Tara rolled off of him and onto the floor. Ryan maneuvered to his side and off his aching bum. He propped his head on his hand. "How did it happen? The car accident, I mean."

Tara sat up, curling her legs under her. "It was right after graduation. A graduation party actually." She pushed a loose tendril of hair behind her ear. "I was drunk. The driver was drunk, and we hit a tree."

Ryan winced. "But you have burns. Did the car catch fire?"

Tara nodded. "I got in a fight with some guy over a bottle of rum as we were leaving. The alcohol ended up spilling all over me and burning in the fire. Most of the burns only left scarring, but my bra melted to my skin and that damaged more tissue. I got breast implants because I couldn't imagine not being whole. Sometimes I wish I'd never done it."

Ryan touched her hand, feather-light. "But wanting to be as much of yourself as you could, I understand." He slapped his knee. "If there was a surgery to fix this, I'd be there yesterday."

"You need your knee to function. I was stuck on vanity. They did help me get a cheerleading position, but when the uniforms changed—" She outlined the cut of the new tops. It was hardly more than a bra. "My scars showed, and that wasn't going to fly."

"With you or with them?"

"Them. I'm okay with people seeing them now. It took awhile. But during the auditions, I was fine, even a bit encouraged, you know. I wouldn't be hiding them anymore. I could push off the persona of a ditzy blonde and show how hard I had worked. They cut me off before I even started the routine." She brushed a speck of dust from her skirt. Her fingers trembled, belying the calmness with which she related the details of her accident and the life-changing aftermath.

He knew the agony of the initial event, but had no idea how to navigate life beyond. From what he could see, Tara had overcome the adversity. She'd found a new career path and a mentor and boss who believed in her. This thing with Chuck was simply a hurdle she would leap over. He wished he could show her how strong she was. If only he could resurface as valiantly. He reached for her hand and squeezed it.

"What happened to the driver?"

"He walked away with a couple bruises." She rolled her eyes and the unfairness of the accident grated on Ryan.

Flashes. Tara's face. Where he remembered her name. He and his friends had crashed a bonfire after graduation. It had been halfway between Glendale and Carterville. He'd lost his friends shortly after they arrived as his attention had been captured by a gorgeous blonde. His gaze had followed her as she flitted from group to group. She was always surrounded by people, and he couldn't summon the courage to approach her. She was the spark for the bonfire.

His heart had fallen when a muscled meathead had slung his arm around her shoulders and planted a slobbery kiss on her cheek. She'd wrapped an arm around his waist as he'd propelled her toward the makeshift parking lot on the edge of the trees. She'd swung a bottle out of the grasp of a friend as they passed by. She and the Neanderthal had alternated swigging from the bottle, and Ryan could tell by their staggering steps this wasn't the first they had imbibed during the evening.

The couple stumbled against the door of the car. The jock climbed in, and the girl moved around to the passenger side.

Ryan started running toward them. He arrived as the engine roared to life, and she reached for the door handle. He slammed his hand on the door, holding it closed.

"What are you doing?" the girl yelled over the noise of the party, shaking the bottle of rum at him. The spicy smelling liquid sloshed and splashed on him.

"You can't get in the car." He butted his hip against the door and the caveman pounded his fist against the window behind Ryan's butt.

"Get out of here! Tara, let's go!"

Up close, she was even more beautiful. Her hair shimmered in the firelight and her skin glowed. Ryan could barely think. He grabbed for the bottle clasped in her hands, but she fought back, jerking his whole body toward her when he didn't relinquish his grip. Ryan only wanted to keep her out of the car. As they battled, the rum splashed over them both. Finally, Ryan managed to yank the bottle out of her grasp, but the victory was as empty as the bottle. The remaining alcohol whooshed out and covered her shirt. He'd had only a brief second to enjoy the view of her drenched top when stars exploded in front of his eyes.

Ryan shifted to a sitting position on the tile. He touched the strange bend in his nose. "You had a wicked right."

Tara's eyes narrowed. "What do you mean?"

"I think I'm the one you fought with over the rum. You broke my nose."

"You couldn't have been at the party." Her hands slid to cover the scarred portion of her abdomen.

"My friends and I snuck over from Glendale and crashed it. I can't believe you're her." How had he not seen it before? His dream girl was right in front of him.

"Her?"

"This girl has been stuck in my head ever since. I only ever heard your first name. I never knew about the crash. I never met another woman as pretty as you until I met you again."

****

Tara blinked and her stomach swirled. She felt like a penny, spinning on its edge, wavering and wobbling about to fall over.

Ryan had been there. Ryan had been the one. If they hadn't fought over the bottle, it wouldn't have spilled on her. She would have walked away from the crash just as unsteadily as the driver had.

She stumbled over to her desk and dropped into her chair. It scooted to the side under her bum, and she flailed for the table to steady herself.

Ryan had been there. Through all the pain, she had been so angry with this faceless person. Every surgery, every failure, she'd dumped at that boy's feet.

He levered himself off the floor with his cane and came toward her. She put her hand out to stop him. She couldn't have him near her right now. She needed to think, to sort this all out, but her fatigue refused to let logic connect the dots. "I can't... I can't believe my burns are because of you."

"I was trying to be your knight in shining armor. Anything to get you to look at me instead of that lunkhead behind the wheel. I knew if you got in that car—" He stopped. "There are so many ifs. If you hadn't been burned. If we hadn't fought. If you hadn't gotten in the car. If you hadn't been drinking. If I hadn't crashed the party." He pressed his hands at the edge of her desk, his face inches from hers. His blue eyes held regret. The emotion deeper than when he'd lost his running career. "I should have tried harder. I failed."

"If I hadn't been burned, my body would be whole." She wanted to rip her shirt open, so he could see the twisted skin in harsh glare of the fluorescent lights. She knew he understood what she had lost. His choice had led her to breast implants which invited men like Chuck to treat her as if they were the only part of her that mattered.

She looked at him, wishing she could grab the anger and regret that had boiled for years and throw it in his face, but his words shoved it away, leaving scuff marks on her heart. It was easier to blame a nameless stranger than accept her poor choices. It was easier to attribute the entire accident to Ryan's actions rather than her inebriated decisions. It was easier to look for escapes than to accept responsibility. It was easier to believe she was a dumb blonde that guys pushed around than prove her intelligence.

She opened her mouth as Ryan pushed away from the desk. How did she explain all that? "I can't—" She didn't know how to finish the sentence, but when she saw his expression, it didn't matter. He was leaving. He grabbed his cane and limped out the door.

Chapter Twenty-Two

Tara awoke face down in her bed to her alarm squawking six o'clock in one ear and her phone jingling in the other. She lifted her face off the pillowcase to find her makeup had left a smeared outline on the fabric. After slapping the off button on the alarm, she turned to the phone and squinted at the caller ID. Minnie? Goodness, why was she calling at this hour?

Then the events of the last twenty-four hours came rushing back. Charles. No, she grimaced, Chuck. And Ryan. *Oh boy.*

She flipped the phone open. "Hello?" she croaked, wondering how her breath hadn't burned a hole through her pillowcase.

"The jerk-wad is still up in his room, complaining about a sore neck. I don't expect he's none too happy with his stay at The Lilac Bower. Been having a problem with the water heater. It cut out right as he jumped into the shower. That city water is cold this time of year. Probably heard him scream halfway to Glendale."

The occurrence that Chuck was out of bed at six o'clock could only be attributed to Minnie destroying his chances for sleep. Tara wasn't sure how to reply. 'Thank you' and 'That's not even close to what he deserves' were on the tip of her tongue, but neither seemed adequate.

"I'm working on breakfast. I may have to run to the store though. The milk I've got isn't even close to its expiration date, and I'd rather have something a touch more sketchy."

"He won't drink milk. He likes some fancy Bavarian cream stuff."

"Does it smell like almonds?"

Tara didn't like where Minnie's train of thought was going. Cold showers and that kind of torture she could get behind, but poison was a little too close to jail time. "Minnie, I don't want you and Chuck to be cellmates."

"Good thought. I'll stick with burning the toast and overcooking the eggs. Hank says the insurance adjuster won't be out until Monday to look at Chuck's car since this isn't a priority case or anything."

"Thank you, Minnie. If you could keep an eye on him over the weekend, it would help out."

"I've got him covered until the library benefit."

Shoot. Tara had forgotten all about it. Leslie had taken care of their sponsorship months before, but she was still obligated to put in an appearance.

"I guess I'll have to take him along." Tara sighed. All she wanted to do was track down proof he was committing tax fraud, but distractions kept coming up.

"Don't you worry. The Ladies will keep him out of trouble."

Tara hung up, wondering what Mark would have to say about Minnie messing with the water heater. When she tried to program the outdoor sprinkling system in January, she'd had a skating rink over the entire yard until the spring thaw.

At least Minnie had a hold of Chuck for now, a situation worse than prison in his case. Tara could balance the rest of her spinning plates. Her job, tax fraud, Ryan, and confiding in

Leslie about all of the above.

If Mark was being his usual gatekeeper self, Leslie wouldn't have heard the news. But Tara couldn't keep it from her. Leslie resurrected the tax office from a collapsing building into a flourishing business. As her friend, Tara couldn't hide the danger she had put the enterprise in. She'd do everything possible to prevent Chuck from doing any permanent damage.

But cleaning herself up was the first priority. She ducked into the bathroom and almost fell in the toilet when she saw her reflection. Her mascara had not only smeared all over her pillow, it left bruise-like smudges around her eyes with streaks down her cheekbones. Her hair was twisted and ratted on one side of her head into a believable replica of a bird's nest. The other side was plastered against her scalp as if she had stood behind a jet engine while spraying an entire can of cheap hairspray.

She shed her clothes, tossing them in the general direction of the hamper. Slashing back the curtain, she stepped into the streaming water before the warm water had traveled all the way up from the basement to her bathroom. The first splash woke her faster than a triple espresso. She gasped in short puffs, glad Minnie hadn't had the notion to tamper with her water heater, but not shocked enough to feel sorry for Chuck. After shampooing her hair, the water had heated enough to allow her to stand in the flow without freezing the blood in her veins. She zipped through the rest of her toiletry process, swiping the minimum of makeup on, but blobbing a good smear of concealer over the dark circles below her eyes. She twisted her hair into a slick chignon. A glance in the mirror told her the look was passable for three hours of sleep.

Within thirty minutes of peeling herself off her pillow, she had pulled out of the drive-through coffee station and was headed to the office, rehearsing the conversation she needed to have with Leslie. She wished she could do it in person, but that meant closing the office with only a week left in the tax season. As much as she had screwed up so far, she couldn't cost Leslie any more clients. She parked in her usual spot at the back of the office lot and extracted her phone from her purse.

She found Leslie in her contacts and pressed send. Holding the phone to her ear, she prayed Mark would answer and tell her Leslie was sleeping. Leslie's rest was a good enough reason to delay the necessary confession.

Her heart rate spiked when Leslie's voice greeted her. What was she supposed to say? The pictures were flashing in front of her, but she couldn't put words with them. "Leslie, I've screwed up bad."

"Oh dear. Isn't Charlie working out? Do you need me to come in?" Leslie's voice became muffled at the tail end, but Tara could still hear. "Mark, it's Tara. No. I'm fine. Shoo."

"It isn't Charlie. It's Chuck. I called the wrong person."

Leslie's voice was muffled again. "Mark, could you get me a glass of water? Thanks, sweetie." Then her voice became clear again. "You didn't find Charlene's number? Wait, did you say Chuck as in Chuck Silverman?"

"Uh-huh." Nausea swept over her at simply acknowledging her mistake. If only her confession was complete.

"Okay. Okay. He's a jerk, but nothing you can't handle. Keep him at arm's length and keep your pepper spray close. He can help you out, but handle the cash. It wouldn't surprise me if he has sticky fingers. Anyway, it's not the end of the world."

Tara sighed. "There's more. I think he's trying to defraud the government. Actually I'm sure of it." Tara explained about the returns she'd found with the deceased client's social security numbers on them. "Ryan's helping me track down the computer evidence, and Minnie's got Chuck holed up at the Lilac Bower."

She waited for Leslie to scream at her, to fire her,

something.

"I'm so sorry this happened, Tara. I should have trusted you with everything, but I didn't want to overwhelm you."

Tara's lips quivered. She couldn't stand Leslie being nice to her when she had failed so spectacularly. She sniffed. "Please yell at me. Fire me."

"Why? You caught Chuck. He's been pulling dastardly stuff like this as long as I've known him. He deserves to be incarcerated and so much more. After his stay with Minnie, Chuck'll be happy to go to prison. She better not mess with anything in the basement though. It took Mark weeks to straighten out the sprinkler thing. You've got everything covered. Keep me posted on what's happening."

Tara choked back the tears. How could Leslie trust her so much? "But Leslie, there's a week left in tax season. We need someone who can do the complicated returns. Who can I call?" It might have been her exhaustion talking. While she wanted to fix everything, her mind was swirling with the steps she needed to take.

"Tara, you can handle it. It's only four and a half days."

"The busiest four and a half days of the year. I can't do this myself. What about the complicated returns? The amended returns? I've never done any of those." Her panic sizzled, despite her resolve. Leslie always helped her through these things. Tara drew strength from Leslie's confidence. Her hand trembled as she reached for her coffee. The sip of caffeine cleared her head a bit. She needed to focus. One step at a time. Ease the slow tilt-a-whirl of emotions. "Who can I call?"

"You'll get a lot of practice. You've had all the training. You went to the full training seminar last winter."

Tara's palms were sweating. She tucked the phone between her ear and shoulder. She wiped her palms against her skirt. "What if I screw up?"

"You can't do anything worse than what Chuck did."

"Thanks a lot."

"You know what I mean." Leslie paused. "You are a better accountant than Chuck will ever be. He can't even screw up without getting caught. Anything goes wrong, you'll fix it. Just like you have been."

"But it's your business reputation. I can't risk that. You've worked so hard to make it what it is." Tara's stomach lurched.

Leslie's voice sank to a whisper. "Do you want me to come in? I can't be on my feet, but if I prop them up, I can type at the computer. I can be moral support."

Tara wanted to say yes and lean on Leslie, but she knew she couldn't. The doctor hadn't put Leslie on bed rest on a whim. He expected her to follow his orders. 'Stay off your feet' meant no work, not just sit down all day.

"No. I can handle it." She grabbed her coffee and chugged. The burst of caffeine shocked her resolve, but she gave herself an out. "I'll call you if I have any questions."

She'd take everything slowly, study each complicated return and triple check her numbers so she knew she was doing everything correctly. One step at a time. It'd take forever, but she could sleep next week.

Then she remembered she had to prove Chuck had stolen all those identities too. Somewhere she'd squeeze in time to do some investigating, but Ryan was helping her.

Ryan. They'd had quite the conversation last night. He had tried to keep her out of the car, and she had smashed his nose. What did it mean for them? Was there even a 'them' to consider? It was a problem she'd have to worry about later. Her plate was full.

Tara headed to the break room to start the coffeemaker since the cold blast in the shower and the triple espresso from the coffee shop would only last so long. As she pushed open the door, she wondered if Ryan would come back and find something to prove Chuck was behind all this stuff. Would he still be willing to help her? What could his motives be? He'd made it obvious, he was attracted to her. She couldn't deny hers to him. His height, his strength, the sparkle in his eyes had her heart skipping.

His kindness in helping her and being an ear to hear her problems and her mistakes was quickly endearing him to her. She still felt unsettled about their conversation last night. Emotions she hadn't visited, that she had locked away, rose to the surface fighting for her attention. Anger that he'd tried to make decisions for her, but now gratitude that he thought of saving her — a perfect stranger.

How would her life have been different if she had never met him, if she had not been burned? All those ifs he'd talked about. Any time that night, she could have made a better decision. She laughed to herself. She might have spent the last twelve years with Ryan instead of hacking away at her self esteem.

The driver had been charged with driving under the influence. She wouldn't have escaped the eyes of law enforcement for being underage. With a drinking charge, she would have never gotten her cheerleading position. Their criminal records had to be squeaky clean. They wouldn't have overlooked her indiscretion.

Ryan wasn't to blame for all the ways her life hadn't turned out as she envisioned. She had made those choices. Ryan deserved a thank you for looking out for her, but first she'd have to apologize for punching him in the face.

She went around the office preparing for the day ahead, arranging coffee supplies, extracting the client files needed and stacking the fraudulent returns into a separate pile. Hopefully, they would be able to prove Chuck was behind those or the IRS would be coming after her.

The phone rang. Tara picked up the receiver and pressed it to her ear.

"Hey, Tara, this is Mark. Leslie and I are heading back to the hospital. Her contractions started again."

Tara gave the usual concerns for Leslie's health and safety and hung up the phone. While she tried to remain calm for Mark, inside she was kicking herself with football cleats. Why hadn't she waited to tell Leslie about Chuck? She should have kept it to herself until Chuck was behind bars. Her hand shook and the ear piece clattered against the desk. Every contraction was her fault. If something happened to the baby, Tara would never forgive herself. All she could do was save the accounting firm.

Chapter Twenty-Three

Bells. As he floated through the last curve of the course. Blurry crowds cheered and shook cowbells. He was running as fast as he could, but the soles of his shoes were covered with chewed gum. He couldn't move his feet forward, and he could feel the pack huffing behind him. Their feet skimming the pavement as they whipped by him. More bells. Then he could hear individual voices. Tara. She'd come to his race? But why was she cheering about deductions and Schedule-C's?

The dream faded, replaced by pain and achiness. His neck was cricked and his left foot numb. He tried to shift his leg to the floor and sit up. Pain burst through his leg like a lightning strike. He bit his tongue to stifle the howl and flopped back on his bed. How long had he slept? The curtains darkened his room to twilight, so he didn't have the sun as an indicator. As sore as he was, it could have been days.

He closed his eyes, working his toes in the exercises he had learned in physical therapy. Slowly the muscles became malleable. He braced, properly this time, and swiveled his legs off the bed. After planting his feet on the floor, he searched for his cane. It had slipped halfway under the bed when he dropped it last night. He gripped the handle and forced himself to his feet. With all the pops and cracks his body made someone overhearing would think he was eighty instead of thirty.

He hiked across the room and found his watch on his desk. Mid-morning. He wagged his head from side to side, surprised by the soreness from hunching over the server the night before.

Tara. He winced as he rubbed his aching neck. Just when things were starting to go right there, he'd screwed them up. Actually, he'd screwed them up before he'd even started. His attempting to help had caused her burns. He failed miserably at protecting her and all he wanted to do was love her. What did he do now? He leaned on the dresser and stared at the yellow and green bruise blossoming around the road rash on his chin. Waltz up to her desk, fall on his knees — well, sit gingerly in the chair next to her — and declare his undying love?

"Ryan, are you up?" his mother called from downstairs.

Depended on her definition of the word. He'd fallen into bed fully-clothed, so he was presentable enough for his mother. "Yeah."

His mother clomped up the stairs and eased his door open. She swung the plastic-covered hanger over her shoulder and dangled a tuxedo in front of him. "Your tuxedo for the library charity event tonight." She hung it on the hook on the back of the door. "I had them let out the leg, so you'll have more room for your brace. You may want to bring a change of clothes or your swim trunks."

Ryan limped over to the penguin suit, barely able to hide his disgust. Thick, itchy, heavy fabric. The only suit he should be wearing was a track suit. "Why do I need swim trunks?"

"I signed you up for the dunk tank from ten to ten-fifteen." She waved her hand and breezed out of the room, leaving Ryan to stare after her with his jaw hanging open.

How was he supposed to help Tara catch Chuck if he was dressed like a penguin and trapped in a dunk tank? He headed for the bathroom, then stopped. That is, if she wanted his help. His track record wasn't stellar in that department. But years of training taught him it wasn't time to throw in the towel.

If he brought a peace offering of food, maybe she'd let him through the door. He pick up some lunch. He swung by Bart's and resorted to a variety of things from the menu. He knew Tara liked the cheeseburgers and fries, but they weren't good for her extended health and he found he was quite concerned about how long she lived, provided he was somewhere in the picture, of course.

He entered the office while she was engaged with a client. He waved the bags of food, then slipped back to the break room. His jacket still hung from the back of the chair where he'd left it the previous night. A quick glance at the server told him it was running optimally. At least he'd done one thing right.

He returned to the office as Tara was finishing with the last customers before closing. She ushered them out a few minutes later and sank onto the futon. "What a morning. I've got two huge returns and they're new customers, too, so I can't crib off last year's returns." She pressed her palms against her forehead. "And the whole time I'm talking to them, I'm thinking how I will prove I didn't cheat the IRS."

"We'll figure it out," Ryan said as he unloaded the bags of food on the small table and handed Tara the paper-wrapped cheeseburger. She shucked the paper and bit into the sandwich.

Cradling the burger, she closed her eyes and took a slow breath. "I'm sorry for punching you. You were trying to help me make a better choice. Thank you for caring. Last night — "

Ryan stopped unwrapping his chicken sandwich when her fingertips grazed his hand. "Last night was intense."

"So much came to the surface and I could hardly process it all. I can't blame you for my decisions. I can't believe you came back." She took a bite of her sandwich. "And thank you for this."

"I couldn't stay away if I tried. So we're good then?" The rest of his life might be riding on her answer. Broken pieces were fitting together to form a picture he'd never imagined.

"Yeah." She laughed. "I think we are."

Ryan let out a breath he didn't realize he'd been holding. Tara was his constant lately — he couldn't lose her.

"Did you find anything last night?" She demolished the sandwich in a couple bites, so Ryan nudged the salad toward her.

"It's not much. As far as I can tell, he didn't do any of those returns under the login created for him."

"He couldn't, because he wouldn't have access to those files."

"Right. The problem is he did them under Leslie's login or yours and while there are time stamps for everything, you were also in the office at those times."

"Unless I was running errands…"

"But do you have proof of any of those?"

Tara scratched her head. "I might be able to scrounge up a receipt or two, but most of the time he asked for them back. Smart thinking on his part. The IRS could still pin the rest on me or think we were working together." She shuddered at the thought.

"I know. There's got to be a way around it."

Tara unsnapped the lid for the salad and wrinkled her nose. She grabbed the packet of dressing and squeezed it on.

"Do you know how much fat is in that?" Ryan asked as she squished every drip out.

"If I'm going to spend the rest of my life in prison, does it matter?"

"It's a white collar crime. I don't think you'd get more

than five years. Martha Stewart is already out."

"Five years. I could be saggy and gray by then."

Ryan couldn't imagine anything about Tara being saggy. But he also knew he'd like to see her in five years. And every day in between.

"I don't see any way out of this unless Chuck confesses and there's about as much chance of that happening as me not eating the chocolate shake you're hiding over there."

Ryan inched the condensation-covered cup forward on the table. It left a streak of water behind it. "Maybe you should hire a lawyer."

"I can't afford a lawyer."

"You'll probably need one before this is all said and done."

Tara sighed. "You're right. Unless I can convince Chuck to confess."

"Chances of which are somewhere between slim and none."

"You're so encouraging." Tara picked up the shake and took a long pull from the straw. "How do you feel about enhanced interrogation techniques?"

"You aren't planning to water-board him, are you?"

"Tempting, but no. There's a mechanical bull and a dunk tank at the library charity event tonight. We get him on one of them and not let him off until he spills the beans."

"He's going to spill something all right," Ryan said. "We'd have to get him drunk first, because I can't see Chuck hopping on a mechanical bull without some liquid courage."

"We can't get him too drunk or his confession won't be admissible in court." Tara rose from her seat on the futon and started pacing around the break room. "We bring witnesses. I'm sure Minnie and her friends will help us out."

"Wait! I've been working on this mobile app for recording. We could give it a try. I was thinking it would appeal to college students trying to record their lectures, but we could get Chuck's confession on it. It's supposed to filter out background noise. It might work." Ryan leaned back in his seat. "I'm still skeptical about getting Chuck on the mechanical bull though."

A smile eased on Tara's lips and her eyes darkened. A little sparkle glimmered in their corners. Her fingertips slid across the v-neck of her blouse and Ryan was sure the temperature in the room jumped ten degrees. She sauntered toward him, her hips swaying enticingly. "There are ways to convince him." She placed her hands on the arms of his chair and leaned forward. It was all Ryan could do to keep his eyes on her face. She looked into his eyes and wiggled her eyebrows, and sweat broke out on Ryan's forehead. He put his hand behind her head and pulled her mouth to his.

She wouldn't do that walk for anyone else.

Chapter Twenty-Four

A rush of heat greeted Tara as she stepped through the doorway to the reception hall. The charity fundraiser for the library was in full swing. The Ladies Night Out had done it again.

The reception hall was decorated as a summer carnival. Side show booths surrounded the hall while games and food booths filled the center. Here and there, chairs, tables, and benches provided resting places between the entertainments. One booth encased in red velvet curtains was completely closed up, and Tara wondered if one of the sponsors had fallen through at the last minute.

At least half the town mingled under the multi-colored lights and covered banners. Tara barely had a moment to wonder what they covered, when Chuck's hand at her back slipped a couple inches too low again. She jumped forward, but she could still feel his cooties creeping on her skin.

She swung her coat off her shoulders and handed it to the waiting attendant, revealing her full length, silver-sequined gown. It had a deep v-neck that mesmerized Chuck and a slit in the side that rose higher than most of her cheerleading skirts fell.

Chuck whistled appreciatively. "You are wasting yourself in an office."

Tara took another step away and scanned the crowd for Ryan. It took her a moment to find him because his back was to her. Then she had to make sure she kept her mouth from gaping open. Since she'd only ever seen him in workout clothes, the transformation was astonishing. The black tuxedo accentuated his tall frame and lean body. It was probably a good thing he wasn't standing at her side because she would have melted into a pool of jelly.

A whiff of Chuck's presence stiffened her spine. "Where's the bar?" he asked as he fussed with his cuff-links again. She wanted to yell that yes, she'd seen the diamond studs, but then she'd add she'd also seen the rainbow reflections proving they were fake.

"I believe it's over on the left." She gestured to the back corner of the hall, her eyes resting on the mechanical bull. It had been trucked in from the seediest bar in the county at Bubba's request and was affectionately known as Sweet Georgia. Bubba was sponsoring it and pledged to donate a dollar for every second a rider stayed on its back. Sweet Georgia's location next to the alcohol guaranteed Bubba's pockets would be lighter by the end of the evening. Minnie knew her stuff with these shindigs.

Chuck slipped into the crowd and wove his way to the end of the line at the bar. It was a relief to not have him breathing down her neck for a few moments. She took a minute to breathe air not clogged with his cologne. In order to get him to confess, she was going to have to stick to him like unpasteurized cream cheese to a gluten-free bagel. Not exactly how she wanted to unwind on a Saturday night, but it'd save her evenings for the next five to ten years.

Minnie swanned up to her and looped her arm through Tara's. She was gowned in an iridescent blue, one-shouldered number with a floor-length skirt that swirled when she walked. If Tara was in half as good of shape as Minnie was at seventy, she'd have done something right in her life. Minnie had the body of a fifty-year-old and moved like perfume on a breeze. "You look lovely, dear. You'll have every eye on you tonight."

There was only one set of eyes she wanted on her tonight and she hadn't connected with him yet. Minnie read her mind. "Yvonne's been dragging him around all evening." Her voice dropped to the whisper. "Is everything all set?"

Tara shook the patent leather clutch she had tucked under her arm. "Ryan loaded the eavesdropping app on my phone. I have to get Chuck bragging."

Minnie nodded to Chuck as he threaded his way back toward them, a flute of champagne in each hand. "He's making the heavy lifting a bit easier." Minnie disappeared as Chuck handed a glass to Tara.

She thanked him and took a tiny sip. Champagne went to her head way too easily, and she needed a tight rein on whatever wits she had.

Chuck poured half the glass down his throat.

"See anything to tickle your fancy?" Tara asked.

His eyes slid over her as smoothly as if they were oiled with the gel in his hair. They stalled on the bottom of the V. He licked his lips.

I walked into that one, didn't I? She inched her way into the throng of people, nodding to customers and friends as she worked her way over to Sweet Georgia. If she couldn't get Chuck on the bull, she'd still have the dunk tank as a backup. She cast a look over her shoulder, trying to locate the tank. It was across the reception hall from the mechanical bull. The mayor had donned flowered swim trunks and was taking his turn in the tank. Somehow he'd gotten out of wearing his tux in the tank. The councilmen were lined up, waiting to throw and tossing friendly jibes at him. A woman in a teal ball gown heaved the baseball toward the target. It crashed into the bulls-eye and a bell clanged. The 'hunk' in the tank splashed into the water and came up sputtering.

Chuck stopped at a high table a few feet from Sweet Georgia. "How long do you have to stay at this shindig?"

"Since Knotts Accounting is a sponsor, I have to be here for the duration." It had better not take the whole night to weasel his nefarious deeds out of him.

Tara pointed to Sweet Georgia, idling in its pen. "Care to take a ride? You could probably break the record."

"There's not enough alcohol in this place to get me on there."

If he found out Leslie was sponsoring the drinks, he might change his mind.

We shall soon find out. Tara waved to a waitress who slalomed through the tables and parked right in front of theirs. After snapping her gum and giving Chuck a thorough going over, which ended with a raised eyebrow, she lifted Chuck's empty glass onto her tray. "Can I get you another?"

Chuck requested another champagne and the waitress left, swooping around a man stumbling toward Sweet Georgia.

When Tara recognized who the drunk was, she was sure of one of two things: either everything would work out perfectly and Chuck would leave the benefit in the back of a police vehicle, or she'd be chasing him down and hauling him back to the Bower. Chuck had been terrified of Hank and Bubba last night; their presence could entice Chuck to say anything to escape.

Hank shucked his tuxedo jacket and climbed on the bull. He adjusted his leather vest and rolled up the sleeves of his dress shirt. Once in the seat, he nodded to the operator. Hank wrapped his hand around the handle. The rear of the bull kicked up and Hank slipped forward, almost sliding face first over the front of the ox. He regained his balance as it jerked back only to lose his grip and tumble off the side onto the floor.

Chuck laughed and Tara could tell it wasn't out of enjoyment. He was ridiculing the country yokels and their entertainments. "Looks like they slowed it down to keep the rednecks on longer."

"They *are* trying to raise money for the library."

The waitress brought Chuck's champagne. He folded a twenty and tucked it into the cleavage of her gown.

"I'm surprised you're still here," Tara said.

He took a drink, made a face of surprise, and took another. "While my tastes are generally," he wrinkled his nose at the surrounding patrons, "more upscale, I know how to have a good time." He downed the champagne in a gulp and held up the glass for another.

This could be bad. If he started to enjoy himself, she wouldn't be able to torture a confession out of him. Her hands started to shake. She excused herself to use the ladies' room in an attempt to regroup. Would her plan still work if Chuck was willing to roll with the punches?

She ducked into the darkened hallway right off the main reception hall and someone grabbed her arm. She knew instantly it was Ryan by the electricity zipping through her. She allowed him to pull her close. Just being near him settled her mind. Well, until she got another good look at him in his tuxedo. If she had been worried about her knees melting before, she needed his cane to stay upright now.

"You clean up pretty good." She smoothed the lapel of his jacket. He smelled clean, fresh from a shower. It was a refreshing contrast from the cologne-soaked fog of Chuck.

"You're not so bad yourself. That dress is something else." Ryan's gaze briefly slid down the sparkles, then back to her eyes. "Simply amazing." He pressed a kiss to her forehead and lightly brushed one of the curls tumbling around her face. "I don't want to mess up your makeup."

Tara blushed. The fantasies flooding her mind wouldn't have left a sequin on her dress, let alone her lipstick flawless. She pulled his lips down to hers and let the carnival fade. Music swirled around them, but the voices disappeared. It was just the two of them. The touch of his body to hers cleared the agitation in her mind and moved the swirling to her heart. All she wanted was to stay in this moment forever, forget about the rest of the tax season, forget about Chuck, and forget about the prison sentence looming. She broke away.

"This isn't going to work. I'm going to screw it up. He's going to take off." She clutched her purse and double-checked her phone was inside. Before she'd left home, she'd charged it and put it in her purse, but she still worried something would go wrong. The battery would drain too quickly, the app wouldn't load, she would forget to turn it on, or her phone would explode.

Ryan raised his head to look into the crowded ballroom. "I think he's going to stick around. He's flirting with some girl who thinks lace over a bikini is a dress."

Tara followed his gaze. "She thinks she's found her sugar daddy."

"If we can't get him to confess, maybe she can." Ryan lifted Tara's chin so she could see into his eyes. "You can do this. Pull your phone out and pretend you are texting. Everything he says will be recorded." He pressed his lips to her forehead again. "Chuck Silverman is no match for you. You have more brains in your little finger than he has in his whole head."

Exactly what she needed to hear. Tara squeezed his hand, then braced her shoulders and made her way back through the crowd to Chuck. In her absence, he had acquired another barely legal admirer, who had also misinterpreted black tie as beach wear. But then, Minnie thought it included a dunk tank, so Tara might be the one doing the misinterpreting. After the last few weeks, it was more than possible.

Chuck was enchanted. The co-eds focused on his sparkly cuff-links and diamond-studded Rolex. Tara was pretty sure it was fake, too. The X looked suspiciously like a K.

Chuck saw her and waved her back to the table. "Meet my new friends, Bebe and Angel."

The girls gave Tara glowing, glassy-eyed smiles, and Tara felt older than the hills. Had she been like these two as a cheerleader? Blonde, bubbly, and out to have fun. Now she was fighting for her reputation and to keep her backside out of jail for the foreseeable future.

The table held four more glasses: two empty and two half-full. She may not have to keep up with the drinks. The girls could match his alcohol intake while she asked the probing questions. One thing was going her way.

"Fabulous, so glad you could join us." Tara gestured to empty chairs at the next table. Bebe and Angel scooted the chairs on either side of Chuck and plopped down, their attention completely diverted by his over-whitened smile and well-oiled locks.

"Chuck here is a partner in an accounting firm and drives a Mercedes," Tara said, adding a few inches to his perceived pedestal.

"Oooh!" Both girls swooned and inched closer to Chuck.

His chest swelled and he upped the charm to gag level. Tara opened her purse and pulled out her phone. Chuck and the girls kept blathering on, so she pretended to be checking her messages. She found the recording app and activated it. It worked! She stifled a squeal. One step down. She pressed the record icon and it flashed. Step two was a go. After placing the phone face down on the table in front of her, Tara said, "Chuck is so brilliant with taxes. He could get you a lot of money."

"You could?" the one Tara thought was Bebe asked. "I had to pay last year. I wasn't going to do them this year." She waved her hand as if filing her taxes was as unimportant as dressing for the weather.

"Yeah." Angel giggled. "Why would the government care about us?"

If possible, Chuck's self-confident smile grew. "Bring your forms to me on Monday. I'll fix you right up."

"You could get us some money?"

"Definitely." Chuck grinned his smarmy smirk, and the girls ate it up.

It couldn't be that easy, could it? He was offering to defraud the government for... well, Angel and Bebe didn't have a lot to bargain with. Shame on her for expecting Chuck to be a little more shrewd. She scanned the crowd for Ryan. She found him beside his mother and an older, rotund gentleman. He gave her a thumbs-up and she nodded. He smiled and it tickled right down to her toes.

"But don't you need some deductions to get money back?" Tara asked. Chuck didn't need much rope to hang himself, but she wanted to make sure he had plenty.

"Deductions, dependents, they're easy enough to come up with." Chuck winked at her, then nodded to the girls. "Easy-peasy."

"You know, I would love some tips. I get so confused when I'm working on tax returns. I'd like to make my clients happier." Tara hated the sound of her voice, the airhead stereotype, but getting Chuck to incriminate himself a little more wouldn't hurt. She let out the rope another yard. "How do you do it?"

"You have to make sure you put a little aside for yourself, too. You're sitting on a gold mine at that tax office. All those closed records and inactive social security numbers. It's not hard to fudge things with the IRS. They don't check things," Chuck said as if explaining a simple procedure to an alien. "All you need is a few social security numbers. You can file returns either in their name and direct the refunds to your P.O. box or add them as dependents to another return. It's simple.

The IRS never catches on."

I guess Chuck has never heard of an audit. Tara took a sip of her champagne. *Or a newspaper.*

"Wow. Have you done this before?" Angel asked. She leaned so hard on the table it almost tipped. The champagne glasses wobbled. Tara grabbed her phone to protect it from an accidental bath. Ryan had reassured her the recording was automatically forwarded to a server, but drenching the phone still made her nervous.

"Sure." As if committing identity theft was no big deal. "Everyone does it."

Tara couldn't believe he kept going. He'd made himself three nooses already, what was one more? "I've been helping out here in Carterville, and I've got over fifty thousand dollars coming to me."

Fifty grand? She stifled a whistle. She hadn't taken the time to add up all the fraudulent returns. Good thing she'd found it when she did.

They had to keep Chuck occupied until the police could be rounded up. At least one of the detectives had to be lurking around here somewhere. From the look of Chuck's companions, keeping his attention shouldn't be a problem.

She tapped out a text to Ryan. He pulled his phone out of his pocket, said something to his mother, then disappeared into the crowd.

Chapter Twenty-Five

Ryan gazed longingly at the bench a few feet beyond his mother. He hadn't been on his feet this long since his surgery. She animatedly discussed final plans for an unveiling with Minnie, but he had tuned out their conversation. As his mind wandered, his eyes found Tara at a high table with the two girls and Chuck. The silver dress she wore was dazzling. It swept around curves he could only hope to become better acquainted with. He didn't see how every male eye in the place wasn't mesmerized by her.

Then his phone buzzed in his pocket. He moved his cane to the other hand and fished the phone out of his breast pocket. A quick glance at the display told him Tara's mission had been successful. His job was to find someone from the police department while she made sure Chuck didn't leave.

Relieved the confession had been secured so early in the evening, Ryan scanned the room for someone in uniform. There might even be time to relax. Or time for something else. Her spangly gown was sparking all kinds of ideas in his imagination.

As he surveyed the crowd, he hoped the software had

been able to capture all the details. They wouldn't be able to check the recording until later tonight. He was glad for Tara's sake things were finally going right. Even though she was scared about doing all those returns by herself, she would be fine. They would certainly be easier without Chuck's pestering.

Ryan tucked the phone back in his pocket. No uniforms stood out, but he was thankful for his slight height advantage over the majority of the attendees. His search would be easier. As he headed for the center of the room, he saw a booth near the dunk tank sponsored by the police department. A reasonable place to start.

He'd traversed a short distance when Mr. Tubbs crossed his path again. He appeared even more uncomfortable in his tuxedo than Ryan was. His cummerbund cinched his girth as tightly as a sausage, and his buttons threatened to rip through their holes. Ryan had spoken briefly with Mr. Tubbs earlier, but hadn't given him a definitive answer to his part-time coaching offer. He needed a little more time to find a reasonable excuse.

"I wanted to speak with you privately," Mr. Tubbs said, blocking the narrow passage between two groups of people, so Ryan couldn't flee.

"I'm sorry I haven't gotten back to you about the coaching job. I—" Ryan studied the tip of his shoe. The shiny black leather was strange on his feet. When had he worn shoes that weren't athletic in nature? Would he ever see himself in the mirror and recognize the person there? The cripple with the cane instead of the lean athlete. Not the image of a successful coach.

Mr. Tubbs waved his hand. "A part-time gig is hardly worth your time, I know. I understand. I do have good news though. It might make your decision easier."

Part-time wasn't the problem. The location and subject matter was. "I don't know." He scanned the room again. No one in uniform stood out. How was he going to find a police officer if Mr. Tubbs yakked his ear off all night? With those two bimbos flirting with Chuck, Tara could only keep them entertained here for so long. They'd be interested in pursuing other activities soon.

"Have a seat and hear me out." Mr. Tubbs tugged him over to a bench and gestured for him to sit.

Ryan didn't want to have this conversation now, but his knee couldn't turn down a rest. He sank onto the bench, and Mr. Tubbs thumped down next to him. The wooden slats squawked, and Ryan grabbed the armrest, sure the bottom of the seat was going to surrender.

"The athletic conference is after us to add another girls' sport in the fall. We had a water polo team, but we're not getting the numbers we used to. They're willing to give us a grant to start a girls' cross country team. We only need five girls to participate for a scoring team. But…" He swung a penetrating stare at Ryan. "I need a coach."

Ryan shifted and twisted his cane in his hand. He started shaking his head. More running, even closer to marathoning. On a track the distances were shorter and the races confined to the oval. In cross country, training would take them all over town. Races spread over a mile or more. How could he keep up with runners while they were competing? And how could he coach without being able to pace his athletes?

"Before you answer… I've been working with the budget and, with Coach Chambers sticking with football, we can swing a more generous stipend." Mr. Tubbs tapped him on the knee. "Don't answer tonight. Let me know on Monday."

On Monday, his answer wouldn't be any different, but he let the athletic director wander away. This wasn't the time or place to spell it out. He could only think of one reason to take the coaching position, but unless he got a move-on, she would be heading off to jail.

Mr. Tubbs had disappeared into the crowd when Ryan's

phone buzzed in his pocket. He checked it to find a text message from Tara that Detective Gager was at the skee-ball games. Ryan searched the room until he found the alleys being dominated by a blonde in a green chiffon gown. An overstuffed green bear lounged at her feet. She swung her arm back and let the ball fly up the alley. It hit the lip and shot straight in the small hole in the center. Bells jangled and a siren light on the top of the machine spun with red and blue flashes. She grabbed the bear by the ear and danced in a circle. "I got the high score!"

The attendant brought her a matching blue bear. She wrapped her arms around them and squealed.

Ryan levered himself off the bench and approached her then. "Having a good night?"

Detective Gager laughed and held up the two bears by their ears. "The kids are going to love these."

"I'm sure they will. Would you be able to put on your detective hat? We have a situation."

"A situation?" Detective Gager tucked the bears under her arm. "Sounds ominous. What's Minnie up to?"

Ryan laughed. "Not Minnie. Come this way."

"Is someone in immediate danger?" Her face sobered.

Ryan wanted Chuck dragged out of the hall by his kneecaps, but a few moments more wouldn't matter. He lowered his voice since ears were all around. "I think we have a case of identity theft, and my friend is being framed for it. She can explain more about it. She's keeping tabs on the perpetrator right now."

He stumbled over 'friend.' It wasn't the word he wanted to use to describe Tara. Soul mate, lover, wife all came to mind. But in order to tell her he wanted her to be any of those, he had to keep her backside out of jail.

She shifted the bears. "Okay. I'll toss these in the car and be right back. Where should I meet you?"

Ryan gestured to the table occupied by Tara, Chuck, and

his bimbos. "Over by the mechanical bull."

Chapter Twenty-Six

When Tara looked up from her phone, Bubba was winding his way through the crowd toward them. She guessed his target wasn't her or anyone at her table, but the mechanical bull, Sweet Georgia. Unfortunately, as he neared them, another patron jostled his arm. His beer erupted from his glass and showered Chuck and one of his admirers. The girl screeched, fanning her drenched chest with her manicured fingernails, and gasping as if it had been a bucket of ice.

Chuck leapt from his seat, knocking his chair over so hard the entire area was silenced by the crack of wood. "You've ruined my suit!" He held up his silk tie and beer streamed down from it onto the floor. "This is Italian silk. I paid three hundred dollars for it."

Bubba handed him a wadded up grease rag he pulled out of who knew where. His jeans — another instance of confusion on the meaning of black tie — rode low enough she didn't have to ask boxers or briefs. The answer was none of the above. Tara gagged.

Bubba snorted, and Tara inched away, preparing for him to spit.

"Three hundred bucks for some silky fabric? And people think I'm a moron."

Chuck's face bloomed a blotchy red. "Are you calling me a moron?"

"If the fancy suit fits."

Tara debated about intervening. She had Chuck's confession, but it would probably help to have him alive when the police arrived. If he got into an altercation with Bubba, his survival wasn't assured.

Chuck leaned forward and pounded his fist on the table. He must have imbibed enough to erase his fear of Bubba. "At least I have all my teeth."

Tara barely held her mouthful of champagne. It threatened to shoot out her nose or cascade into her lungs. She slapped her hand over her mouth to hold the fluids in. Despite watering eyes, she managed to swallow, directing the bubbly to her stomach and not her lungs.

Bubba didn't seem to think that was an insult. He grinned, revealing more precious metals than were in Chuck's watch. "Can't keep the ladies away. They know I put my money where my mouth is."

Chuck turned to his companions. "What do you prefer—" he looked Bubba up and down "—a man with money in his mouth or money in his pockets?" Chuck yanked his money clip out of his pocket and flipped it on the table. There was a thick stack of bills encased in a Benjamin. The girls eyed the bundle, probably calculating how far into the night it could get them.

"I will bet you that whole wad I can outlast you on Sweet Georgia," said Bubba. "We'll see who's the man and who's the moron."

Chuck's lip curled in a poor imitation of Elvis. "You're on." He shrugged off his jacket and draped it over the back of Bebe's chair. He winked at his new girlfriends and Tara. "Who are you putting your money on?" he asked with all the charm of a car salesman.

The girls couldn't take their eyes off the roll of bills between their empty drinks. They tittered. "You, of course."

Chuck ignored Tara as he unhooked his cuff-links and rolled his sleeves to his elbows. Tara was glad he didn't demand her opinion. While she figured Bubba would hold out the longest, she couldn't say either man was her version of a man.

Bubba slapped a coin on the table. "Flip for who goes first." He nodded to Tara and she picked up the coin. Chuck called heads, and Tara revealed the coin. "Tails."

Bubba nodded and rubbed his grease-lined fists together. He did some shoulder stretches and arm flexes as he approached Sweet Georgia.

"You forgot to put your money down," Chuck called after him.

Bubba ambled back, eyed Chuck's money and pursed his lips. Then he ran his tongue over his teeth and pushed one gold-edged tooth loose with his tongue. He set the tooth on the table next to Chuck's money.

Chuck turned an unflattering shade of green.

"Okay," Tara said. "I'll watch the bets." *But I won't touch them.*

Bubba returned to Sweet Georgia, grasped the worn handle and swung himself into the seat. The operator offered him a helmet, but Bubba waved it away and gave the go signal.

The rear of Sweet Georgia bucked and Bubba rolled with it, flying his free hand in the air like a flag. After a full minute, it was obvious to Tara and the rest of the crowd they were about to witness mechanical bull riding history in Carterville. The crowd chanted, "Bubba! Bubba!"

As the operator bumped the lever up to the next level, he signaled Bubba had made it to the top level. Bubba's hips rotated as Sweet Georgia rocked and bucked. The bull twisted, and Bubba's rear slipped. The pocket of his jeans caught on the side of the saddle. While Bubba tumbled out of the seat, his jeans did not. The crowd cheered and hooted as Bubba untangled himself from the bull and hitched his jeans back around his non-precious metal jewels.

"Bubba missed the record by a tenth of a second," the operator announced and the onlookers groaned. "Do we have any challengers?"

Chuck downed the rest of his drink, then skipped up to the bull like a political candidate trying to fit in with his constituency. People cheered for him as well. He awkwardly jumped on the bull and wrapped his hand around the handle, also declining the helmet.

Ryan snuck up behind Tara. He placed his hand on the small of her back. "Does he have a shot at staying on?"

"With as many drinks as he's had, I'm surprised he found his way there." She laughed, angling her body toward his. "I'm glad he's wearing a belt."

Ryan laughed. "I think everyone here would be willing to donate for a sturdy one for Bubba."

"Were you able to find a police officer?"

"She had to run out to her car a minute. Hope she makes it back before Chuck kills himself."

The operator was about to start Chuck's ride, when Chuck motioned for him to stop. He said something to Angel — or was it Bebe? — and she brought him her beer. He downed that too and handed the empty back to Angel. He whirled his hand, and the operator started the bull. Chuck's butt bounced off the side on the first rock. He regained his seat, but slipped to the other side on the next one. Chuck swung around like a rag doll for a couple rocks, but managed to keep his grip. The operator bumped him up a level.

"This almost makes all the crap he's given me worth it."

"Except the part where he framed you for identity theft."

"He can't make up for that until I see him in handcuffs."

Ryan surveyed the crowd and his gaze ended at the door. He raised his hand and gestured for someone to come this way. A moment later, the svelte figure of Carterville's only plainclothes detective approached. She'd added a simple black messenger bag to her evening ensemble.

"Detective Gager." She flashed her badge and ID. "You wanted to see me?" The detective gave Tara a suspicious look as she took in the multiple empty glasses on the table and the other two occupants.

She probably thinks she walked into a cat-fight. She gripped her phone and moved closer to the detective. "I have evidence of identity theft and defrauding the Internal Revenue Service."

"Identity theft?" Detective Gager reached in her bag for a notebook. "That's a serious charge. You have to be prepared to back it up."

"Yes, I understand, but the culprit is here, and we have a recording of his confession," Tara explained.

"You said it was urgent. Identity theft isn't life threatening and very difficult to prove. Without seeing the paper-trail to back it up, I can't arrest anyone. Just who do you believe committed this crime?"

Tara and Ryan both tipped their heads toward Chuck, but Tara's heart was sinking. Detective Gager wasn't going to perp-walk Chuck out of the benefit. Tara couldn't let him come into the office on Monday. She had to convince the officer Chuck had committed a serious crime.

Chuck flailed around on Sweet Georgia, having somehow hung on at the highest level, belying the neck injury he'd claimed this morning. His tie flopped around his neck as the bull bucked forward and twisted. Sweet Georgia kicked the rear up and Chuck tipped forward, almost taking a header into the floor, but his white-knuckled grip kept him from toppling into the hay.

"You're kidding," Detective Gager said. "There's no way that man is capable of defrauding the Internal Revenue

Service."

"But we have a recording," Tara insisted, waving her phone.

"Without the paperwork, the confession doesn't mean anything. We need to have the body, so to speak. If you bring everything in to the office Monday, I can look it over then." The detective turned to rejoin the party.

Tara couldn't let her leave without fitting Chuck with a new set of bracelets. There was no way she'd leave him at the office alone tomorrow either. "If you flirt with him, he'll probably offer to fudge your taxes and get you a bigger return. Please stay. He'll fall off the bull any second now."

"He better," Bubba interjected. He jammed his fists into his hips. "I'd hate to lose my favorite tooth." He picked up Chuck's money clip as Chuck took another heart-stopping near-tumble on Sweet Georgia, but somehow clung to the handle. Bubba flipped through the bills and they came loose from the clip, spilling onto the table.

"Now hold on a minute!" Bubba picked up one of the twenties and held it to the light. He wrinkled his nose and slammed the bill on the table under his chipped fingernails. "That crap apple lying—" and Bubba was barreling toward Chuck and Sweet Georgia before anyone had a chance to blink. He ripped Chuck off the bull and flung him to the floor. He jammed his mud-encrusted work boot — another miss on the black tie interpretation — into Chuck's heaving chest. "You were trying to pass fake twenties off in exchange for my real gold tooth!"

Detective Gager grabbed the bill and studied it. "He's right. It's the old style but the ink isn't right. Someone's been passing this stuff all over town." She snatched her phone from her bag and called for backup. Then she scrambled over to where Bubba had Chuck nailed to the floor, fishing in her bag and withdrawing the silver cuffs Tara had been longing to see. Bits of hay clung to Chuck's sweat-soaked shirt and hair as he tried unsuccessfully to thrash away from Bubba's boot and his new genuine stainless steel jewelry.

"You're under arrest for distribution of counterfeit currency." Detective Gager yanked Chuck to his feet and slapped the cuffs on his wrists. Chuck's protests were drowned out by the string of curses and rantings from Bubba.

"Tara," Chuck squeaked. "You gotta help me."

"You got it." She gave him a thumbs-up and he relaxed enough for the detective to ensnare his wrists. "I'll make sure they have all the evidence they need so you can have a nice long stay at the penitentiary."

Chuck's jaw dropped as Detective Gager clapped her hand around his elbow and hustled him outside.

Bubba returned to the table and pushed through the empty beer glasses. "Ah-ha!" He grabbed his gold tooth and wedged it back in his mouth.

Tara grabbed his arm before he disappeared into the crowd. "How'd you know the money was fake?"

Bubba shrugged. "We get them all the time at the junk yard. I'd be out of business in a week if I didn't know what a fake twenty looked like. You know, people who do business with a junkyard ain't always on the straight and narrow." He smirked, revealing his glittering teeth, then winked. "Told you I wasn't the moron."

Chapter Twenty-Seven

Ryan stared after Detective Gager as she hauled Chuck out to the parking lot. Ryan had never been so happy to see the back of someone. He turned to give Tara a high five. One less distraction for her at the office. If she didn't have to chase after all of Chuck's junk, she'd have time to focus on him.

Focus on him? He needed to do something to make himself worthy of her. The job offer from Mr. Tubbs flitted through his head again. It was a job. But one he seriously couldn't handle.

She slapped his hand, then laced her fingers through his and brought their hands down to her side. "I can't believe it worked. Course, I owe Bubba a huge favor."

"After showing us his backside, I'd say we're even." He squeezed her hand.

Tara laughed. "You're probably right. Thank you for your help, by the way. It was nice to know you had my back." She brought the back of his hand to her lips and kissed it.

The touch of her mouth sent a shot to his gut. The way her dress shimmered over her curves had him ready to sprint a mile with her on his shoulders just to get her all to himself.

"Glad to help." He tugged at the collar of his shirt. "Want to skedaddle?"

"Aren't you having fun?" Her eyes glittered enticingly.

Ha! Get him out of this goof-suit and into something more comfortable and he could think of several ways to have more fun. Running over hot coals. Being chased by bees. Watching his mother's aerobics class. But top of the list was sliding Tara out of her spangly dress.

Ryan scanned the crowd, then slid his gaze to Tara. She was the only person or activity he was willing to spend his attention on. His thoughts centered around getting her out of here and somewhere a lot more interesting, preferably without the carnival music. He inched toward the door, but Tara tugged him the other way. Her eyes spun around the room, lighting up at the carnival atmosphere. Ryan sighed. Tara was finally able to enjoy the party. His plans could wait while she had a few hours to cut loose.

"Did you see anyone you know? I'm sure there are some people from Glendale here." She wandered toward the closed red velvet tent. Ryan allowed her to draw him back into the fray. He'd follow the iridescent vision anywhere.

"I did actually. My old athletic director is here. He offered me a coaching job." He shook his head, still befuddled by the proposition.

Tara squealed. "He did? That's fantastic. When do you start?" She threw her arms around his neck. "Isn't this the best night?"

While he enjoyed the feel of her body against his, he couldn't match her enthusiasm about the job.

"What's the problem? This is great news." The excitement wiped from her face. She studied him intently.

Ryan felt like a huge idiot. She was right, he should be thrilled. He should be ecstatic. A job in a field where he had a lot of experience. Unfortunately, he felt worse about bursting Tara's bubble. "He offered me a job developing a girls' cross country team and coaching track for what's left of this season."

"But you turned it down?" She leaned away from him. She gripped his sleeve, her face confused.

He shook his head. "I can't set foot on the track like this." He grasped his cane in the middle and waved it at her. His voice rose, anger over his recent life changes punctuated every word. "How can I coach runners when I can barely walk?"

"I've heard about a coach who chases his team from a golf cart." She jammed her hands on her hips.

"It was a station wagon and he was my high school coach." The last coach he wanted to emulate.

"Seemed to work pretty well for you." Her eyes narrowed, and Ryan wished for a welding apron to block the sparks shooting at him.

"I don't want to step into Coach Chambers' shoes." He'd succeeded in spite of Coach Chambers' methods, not because of them. He'd gained experience and knowledge studying on his own. He'd dreamed of coaching... before his body let him down. But if they were talking about people using their talents...

"What about your college applications? Filled those out yet?" Ryan shot back. "Seems we both have opportunities we aren't willing to take." The second the words left his tongue, he wished them back. This wasn't the time or place to examine their vulnerabilities.

Tara's face reddened, and Ryan was sure smoke was going to puff from her ears. Anything related to running hurt more than jabbing bamboo under his fingernails. The look on Tara's face was ten times worse. He took a deep breath. Tara simply wanted the best for him, but moving on was terrifying. But his terror was no reason to blow up at Tara or throw her fears in her face. He opened his mouth to apologize.

"Oh, Ryan!" His mother's voice whistled through the assembly. "I've been looking all over for you. You're late."

"Late for what?" He didn't need this right now. He

wanted to get Tara alone, so they could straighten this out and get on with more entertaining things. His mother clenched his sleeve and dragged him across the hall.

"The Dunk a Hunk. You were supposed to be in the tank ten minutes ago." She tapped her wrist, then grabbed his.

"Okay. I'll get my swimsuit and be there in a couple minutes." He wrenched his sleeve free, intending to apologize to Tara first, but the look on her face suggested the tank was a safer alternative.

"There's no time. We are losing money every second that tank is empty." She slapped her hands on her cheeks and gasped. "No. No. Your tux will be great. People will pony up extra money."

Ryan barely had time to fish his phone out of his pocket and slough off his coat. He handed them to his mother before she herded him up the steps to the tank. He caught sight of Tara at the bottom of the steps as his mom dropped his tuxedo jacket into Tara's arms and rushed away. If Tara ended up in the tank, she'd boil the water. He hoped a cooling off period would be beneficial for their eventual conversation.

Chapter Twenty-Eight

Tara chased after Ryan and Yvonne, struggling to keep up as the crowd shuffled in front of her. She wasn't done with Ryan and his decision about the coaching job. How could he turn it down?

He would be a natural coach with his knowledge and experience. He'd also be great with the kids. He'd propped her up often enough in the last couple weeks. Didn't he know that?

Tara's emotions were bouncing more than Sweet Georgia. They'd caught Chuck and saved Leslie's company.

But that brief moment of relief had been washed away. What was Ryan thinking? A job offer in a field he knew so much about; he shouldn't even think of refusing. He'd be perfect.

If Ryan didn't take the coaching job, he would be leaving soon. Leaving Carterville and her. It was the only explanation she could come up with. He was leaving her to take a job somewhere else. *Leaving her?* That was it. He thought she was too needy, too airheaded, and he couldn't wait to get away from her. Hadn't she proved she was worth more than superficial interest? She thought they had something real. Something they couldn't find just anywhere.

But Ryan had made no declarations and didn't talk of the future. She'd made all that up on her own. She'd allowed Ryan to con her as much as Chuck had.

She hovered near the front of the line with Ryan's jacket. She looked down at the coat and brushed away a speck of lint. What was she doing standing here like a coat rack? She rolled her eyes. Besides being the idiot everyone thought she was. She chucked the jacket on the floor and took a place at the front of the line.

Tara tapped her foot while Ryan settled in the tank and others lined up behind her for their chance to dunk him. A dollar for three throws at the target. Tara reached for her purse, then changed her mind. She bent and picked up Ryan's coat. After a quick search of the pockets, she found his wallet. Unfortunately, it was devoid of cash. She flipped it closed, then opened it again to peek behind the credit cards. Ah-ha! An emergency twenty. She kept cash hidden to use only for an emergency, too. She slid the bill out of the pocket and crushed it in her fist. If she didn't let off some of this anger and disappointment, it would be an emergency.

She tossed the crumpled bill at the attendant and stepped up to the line.

"How many throws?"

"All of them," Tara said, holding her hand out for the marred softball. She rubbed her fingers over the crusty leather and stared at Ryan. A golden opportunity lost. She wound up and chucked the ball. It went high and wide of the target. Someone behind her made a remark about throwing like a girl. Ryan gave her a thumbs-up. *If he thought that was a good throw, he had another thing coming.* He should think twice about encouraging her. She needed a couple throws to get warmed up. She grabbed the next ball and wrapped her fingers around the seams.

"You should take the job," she muttered as she let this one fly. It dinged the corner of the target, but not hard enough to trigger the release. The ball ricocheted off the tank, and Ryan almost dunked himself when he flinched.

He might have said "what was that?" but Tara screwed up her mouth and reached for another ball. She had been through enough this week with the stress of tax season, Chuck's demands, and Ryan's stupid, stupid obstinacy. "Lead me on, did you?" She whipped the ball at the target. She missed again, this time nailing the acrylic glass surround with a vicious thunk.

"Somebody's got some anger issues," the man behind her said under his breath.

Tara snatched another ball and whirled around on her heels. She shoved the ball under his nose. "Unless you want this ball blocking your next sneeze, you'll keep your comments to yourself."

The man stepped back a full yard and put his hands up to protect his ability to shoot germs from his nose.

"Thank you." Tara pursed her lips and turned back to the tank. She tightened her focus on the red bulls-eye. This time Ryan was hers. She whipped the ball with a caveman-like growl.

If she could discover Chuck's fraud and get him arrested, and save Leslie's company, she had shown she was the competent, strong woman she wanted to be. She could be a serious accountant. She'd be filling out those college applications as soon as tax season ended. She was worth it. If Ryan didn't think that, he could take a swim.

The ball nailed the target with such a clang everyone for thirty yards ducked. Tara caught the gape of surprise on Ryan's face before he tumbled into the water.

She squeezed her eyes shut to hold back the tears that suddenly threatened. Stepping away from the throwing line, she dabbed her eyes so as not to mess up her eye make-up —

at least while she was still in public. Why did Ryan matter so much to her? The realization hit her as hard as one of the softballs she'd been throwing.

She was in love with him.

She dropped away from the dunk tank, ready to disappear into the crowd. In love with him? Why did she have to figure it out the moment after she learned he was ditching her? Maybe she was the idiot. She couldn't stay at the benefit. Before leaving, she took one last look at Ryan. One last image to remember him by.

And what an image it was.

He came up sputtering and gasping, his shirt clinging indecently to his chest. The lean muscles on his arms and hinted at by his shoulders were well-represented through the transparent fabric. Tara's mouth went dry, and her anger faded a smidge.

Minnie appeared in front of the dunk tank, waving her hands like she was directing traffic. While Minnie had everyone diverted, Ryan waded to the ladder and worked his way out of the tank. Yvonne hurried over with a towel and draped it over his shoulders. With Ryan's marvelous abs out of eyesight, Tara's mind started working again. And she remembered why she wanted to smash his head with a softball. After the mess with Chuck was cleared up with the police, she was done with Ryan.

Tara intended to scoot out of the benefit and bring the paperwork over to the police station. They could call Ryan with any questions about his recording application.

"Since I have your attention, we can get on to the headline of our benefit," Minnie announced. "We all love our library and know it is desperately in need of expansion. All the proceeds from this evening's entertainment will go toward the building project. At this time we will begin the silent auction. Bids can be placed in the red tent behind you. Get out your wallets and bid on these!" She waved her hand in a giant flourish. The covers on the hanging banners above them whooshed away on invisible strings. If the audience had been quiet after Ryan's dunking, they were painfully silent now. Everyone's eyes were locked in shock and awe on the over-sized posters. "Place your bids at the red tent. The library needs you!"

Tara squinted at the closest one. It was a well-aged woman posing in the style of a 1950s pin-up girl, all ruffled swimsuits, floppy hats, and voluptuous curves. Each of the posters, while tastefully and coyly posed, featured one of the Ladies Night Out. The woman on the closest poster was in good shape, but she wasn't centerfold material. Was that Minnie? Tara recognized the hat from one of the rooms at the Lilac Bower. It was definitely Minnie. So this was the photo shoot Minnie had been talking about. Either Minnie was a marketing genius, or she had permanently scarred the entire town.

People around Tara gasped, then chuckled and moved in the direction of the tent with comments like "I want number four" or "I want a calendar with all of them" or "These would be great refrigerator magnets." So Minnie was a marketing guru.

Ryan limped to Tara's side. He bent to pick up his cane and leaned his weight on it with a sigh. "Minnie sure can clear a room. What's all the rush?"

Tara cast him a sidelong glance. "Have you taken a good look at *all* the pictures?"

Ryan's towel dropped to the floor as he leaned forward to get a better view of a poster to their right. Tara thought he might follow the towel, when the horrified words erupted from his mouth. "Is that my mom?"

Chapter Twenty-Nine

"How does it feel to be a free woman?" Ryan asked as they traversed the darkened parking lot outside the police station. Detective Gager requested they bring in the evidence after the benefit. Chuck was ensconced inside, awaiting his hearing on Monday morning.

They'd dropped off the corroborating evidence and a copy of the recording, garnering Ryan an offer for a license for the listening application. Tara had lost track of time in the windowless interrogation room and was surprised to see shades of pink lighting the eastern horizon. Thank goodness it was Sunday, and she didn't have to be at the office bright and early.

She was ready to strip off her dress and sink into bed. Ryan was lucky. He'd changed out of his soaked tuxedo and into warm-up pants and a sweatshirt.

"I wasn't actually incarcerated, but having them believe my evidence — with your help, of course — feels pretty good." She stepped toward her car, desperate to put some space between herself and Ryan. When they'd been trapped in the interrogation room explaining the fraudulent returns and the recording system, all she could think about was what she and Ryan might have been.

She and Ryan didn't have what she thought they did.

Ryan caught his cane on a pot hole and stumbled. He wrapped his arm around her shoulders to stabilize himself. "I'm still wobbly on this cane. If I don't watch where I walk, I'll be hanging all over you."

Tara wanted to slip her arm around his waist and feel their steps sync as she knew they would, but she shrugged out of his embrace instead. *I don't mind keeping you close.* But she reminded herself, it would be good to get used to distance between them. More was surely coming.

"It's been a long day." Tara reached for her purse and dug inside for her keys. "I think I'm going to sleep until Monday morning." Her hand wrapped around the key chain and she squeezed the jagged metal into her flesh. The keys jangled as she tried to fit them in the door lock. "Have a good night."

"Can I see you tomorrow?"

She turned her head as he spoke and realized he was much closer than she thought. If she looked into his eyes, he would draw her in. Their kiss in the hallway; her body pressed against his; the faint, enticing scent of his soap; and the comfort of his embrace, all flashed through her mind with longing. If she looked into his eyes, she would only get hurt. She forced her gaze to his chest. "I don't think that would be a good idea."

"Okay — wait, what?"

She was surprised by the confusion in his voice. She kept her eyes locked on the athletic shoe logo on his sweatshirt. Her eyes would betray her soul, betray how much she cared for him, and how it would rip her apart when he left. She didn't dare meet his gaze. A few more minutes, she wouldn't be able to hold back the tears much longer. Her words came slowly as if they were a foreign language she couldn't pronounce. "I don't think we should see each other anymore." Better to cut the ties herself than let him saw away at them gradually fraying every nerve.

Ryan tipped her chin and forced her eyes up to his. "Are you drunk?"

If only she was. Another glass or six of champagne would take the bite out of this evening. "I don't see any reason for us to continue a doomed relationship if you are leaving."

Ryan shook his head in confusion. "I'm not leaving."

"But you're not taking the coaching job in Glendale, so you'll leave when the next job opens."

"I can't coach. I'll find something else." He gestured to the police department. "I can write software from anywhere. Why does it matter what job I have?"

It was the 'from anywhere' that bothered her. It wasn't worth sharing though. Why open herself up for more hurt? Tara sighed. "You'd be so good at coaching."

"I don't understand why you think that. I'd be a more pathetic version of Coach Chambers. Instead of a station wagon, I'd have a limp. At least he was capable of running."

Tara stomped her foot. A coach had to nurture talent, not keep up with it. "You're a hometown hero. The kids will automatically look up to you. You have so much experience to share with them." As she listed justifications that danced around her real reason for wanting Ryan to become the Glendale coach, she asked herself what was wrong with her. At the benefit, she had been angry enough to throw baseballs at his head, and now, she was tiptoeing around the subject.

Tara breathed, letting the oxygen fill every nook in her lungs, then seep slowly out. "If you took the job, it'd mean you were here to stay." Her courage ran out before she could finish with "and I would have a chance with you."

Ryan twitched his cane, shifting his weight onto his bad leg and back to his good one. He looked down at his shoes, then back up at her. "You like having me around?"

Why did he have to be so cute? "You could say that."

"I think I just did." Ryan grinned and a dimple dotted his cheek.

Tara couldn't help but run her fingertip along it and down Ryan's jaw. His five o'clock shadow was like fine sandpaper.

Hope trickled back in. If this last week had taught her anything, it was that she needed to go after what she wanted and to keep moving through the rough spot. If she kept on her feet, step by step, she made it through. She was stronger than she thought. She was stronger with Ryan by her side.

She wouldn't let him go without putting herself out there. "You make me better, stronger. I've learned so much these last few days, but I wouldn't have survived without you beside me. I've been a basket case at times, but when you were around, you gave me calm." The words surprised Tara. Had she really said all that? She couldn't explain those feelings to anyone else. It should feel like she was wavering on the edge of a cliff. Instead she was in a meadow with the sun warming her skin.

Ryan shook his head. "You're going to think I'm crazy, but you've been the same for me. When I've been the weakest, I had to seek you out. Because somehow it would be better when I was with you."

Tara studied Ryan's eyes. She saw the help he was asking for, but couldn't express. "If I can get Chuck yanked off a mechanical bull, you can take the coaching job. We can't afford to be apart." She raised her eyebrows. "Isn't running ninety percent mental? Just because you can't run up Heartbreak Hill doesn't mean you can't teach the kids the mental toughness it takes."

"And if that's like tackling a never-ending Heartbreak Hill?" He trailed his finger along her cheek.

She remembered their discussion about the hill that had ruined Ryan's Boston Marathon experience. They would conquer their hills together. She leaned into his touch and smiled. "Not every marathon is all downhill and I will be right by your side, cheering you through every step. Maybe I'll even dust off my pom-poms."

"It's a deal." Ryan wrapped his arms around her waist. "I think we were made for each other."

Tara leaned her head against his shoulder and knew he was right. The way his arm felt around her, the way they encouraged and supported each other. Whether they were heading up hill or down, they were traveling together.

Epilogue

Ryan stood at the finish line of the track with a stopwatch and a list of split times on a crumpled paper in his hand. His cane was propped against his leg. "You're doing great. Another lap like that last one and you'll set a personal best," he called to the runner who flew past him. She tailed the leader by fifty meters, but was still having the race of her life.

Ryan's throat tightened as he saw determination fill the girl's face and her turnover go just a bit quicker. He wanted to be out there next to her, pacing her through each step. Ryan turned as the girl rounded the curve to the back stretch and dug in as the wind pummeled her face. "Keep pushing! Two hundred meters left."

He could feel each of the girl's steps as if they were his own. The wind lashing his face, the burning gasp in his lungs, and the ripple of force as his feet pounded the track's rubberized surface.

The girl rounded the last turn, her arms pumping as she clawed for the finish line, her last hundred meters a blur of effort until her legs flew across the finish line. She stumbled to a stop, then bent, grabbing her knees to push air into her heaving lungs.

Ryan blinked back tears that misted his eyes. He grabbed his cane and limped over to the girl as she made her way off the track. "Great job!" He patted her shoulder as she stared with her mouth hanging open like a landed fish. "You were right on your targets for all your laps."

"What was my final time?" she wheezed.

Ryan held up the watch, thankful he'd remembered to stop it as the emotions of a race washed over him. The girl glanced at it and shook her head. "That can't be right."

Ryan flipped the display, so he could read the time. "You knocked twenty seconds off your best time. Most of that was in your last lap. Congratulations."

"All I could think about was what you said, Coach. Leave it all out there."

Ryan nodded. He hadn't expected Tara's predictions to come true so quickly. He'd only been coaching for a week. This was his first track meet. Between coaching and tweaking the recording application, his life in Carterville was enough to make a good living, but more importantly, he was enjoying himself. Those first steps onto the track had been more nauseating than toeing the line for his first marathon, but he'd quickly developed a rapport with the girls. They were eager for the attention Coach Chambers hadn't given them and thrived on his tips and stories. Watching them grow was as rewarding as running himself.

Ryan patted the girl on the shoulder and directed her to get some water. The stands were sparsely populated with friends and family of the athletes. Some things never changed. But one person in the stands caught his attention. He went to the fence and called her name. "Tara!"

Tara waved and hopped down the metal steps. She adjusted her baseball cap over her blonde ponytail. She wore a gray hoodie with Glendale scrolled in red across the front.

"Those colors look good on you."

"I'm afraid someone is going to recognize me as a Carterville cheerleader and beat me up for being a traitor."

"I'll ward them off with my cane." He stretched over the fence and kissed her. A couple boys from the team hooted, and Ryan pulled away wondering how he could live without the taste of her lips every day. "I didn't expect you to be here today."

"The office is closed today. After being there until midnight, and making sure all the returns went through, I needed a break. It's beautiful out today. Oh, and I have news!"

"You sound like my mom. She always has news."

"Leslie gave birth last night. A girl. They named her Wendy. She was born at 11:55 — just as tax season ended."

Ryan laughed. "That's just about perfect."

"I thought so, too."

"Weren't they having a boy?"

"Mark mistook the umbilical cord for something else." Tara giggled.

"I see. I thought your news would be about your college applications." He studied her face.

"Mailed them on the way over here. I had the perfect essay topic: When you think you are in over your head. It practically wrote itself." The wind sprayed her ponytail, so the blonde hair glowed like gold in the sunlight. Her eyes sparkled despite how Glendale's red and gray clashed with their lustrous blue. "Oh and the library fundraiser, they're at eighty percent of their goal, and it's only been a week."

Leave it all on the track.

He stuffed the stopwatch and the paper with the splits into his pocket. He reached for the blowing strands of hair and wound them around his fingers, then he gazed into Tara's eyes. "I love you, Tara Mansfield, even when you are in Carterville colors. I can't live another minute without you. Will you marry me?"

She blinked at him for a moment, then sprang over the

fence as easily as an Olympic hurdler. "I thought you'd never ask."

She slipped her arms inside his open windbreaker and planted her mouth on his, squelching his indignation at her impatience. As whistles and catcalls erupted around him, he decided he didn't care about her impatience even a little.

About the Author

I live in the Great Lakes state with my husband, three rambunctious children and two barking Beagles (I suppose that is redundant.) When not suffering the woes of potty training three toddler/preschoolers, I enjoy reading, running (sometimes it's fleeing the craziness at home), reconstructing clothing, thrift store shopping, and surfing Pinterest.com. (I spend way too much time there and am getting all kinds of exciting ideas for projects for my husband to do. He is less than thrilled by this.)

I love writing romance because I enjoy stories where everything works out all right in the end and the main characters have a happily ever after. My stories are set in small towns with quirky characters that take on a life of their own.

Astraea
Press

Pure. Fiction.
www.astraeapress.com